I0681396

Into the Rabbit Hole

Nail in the Coffin

In scientia fidei robur

Nisi qui habet scientiam in fide

Book 8

Books by Micah T. Dank

Into the Rabbit Hole *series*

Book 1: Beneath the Veil

Book 2: The Sacred Stones

Book 3: The Secret Weapon

Book 4: Pangaeas Pandemic

Book 5: The Hidden Archives

Book 6: The Final Type

Book 7: The Unbegun

Book 8: Nail in the Coffin

Coming Soon!

Book 9: The Ultimate Truth

Into the Rabbit Hole

Nail in the Coffin

Book 8

Micah T. Dank

SPEAKING VOLUMES, LLC
NAPLES, FLORIDA
2022

Nail in the Coffin

ISBN 978-1-64540-869-7

To all my supporters out there, this book is for you.
I don't like using the term fan because that's
short for fanatic and I hope none of you are.
I keep writing for you. This is your book.

The first people a dictator puts in jail after a coup are the writers, the teachers, the librarians because these people are dangerous. They have enough vocabulary to recognize injustice and to speak out loudly about it. —Madeleine L'Engle

Preface

A common position expressed by many astrologers sees the Age of Aquarius as that time when humanity takes control of the Earth and its own destiny as its rightful heritage, with the destiny of humanity being the revelation of truth and the expansion of consciousness, and that some people will experience mental enlightenment in advance of others and therefore be recognized as the new leaders in the world.

Proponents of medieval astrology suggest that the Pisces world where religion is the opiate of the masses will be replaced in the Aquarius Age by a world ruled by secretive power-hungry elites seeking absolute power over others; that knowledge in the Aquarian Age will only be valued for its ability to win wars; that knowledge and science will be abused, not industry and trade; and that the Aquarian Age will be a Dark Age in which religion is considered offensive.

Americans live in a world of pseudo-facts, which is created for them by their own media. —Professor Daniel Boorstin (Librarian of Congress, 1975-1987)

Chapter One

"911, what's your emergency?" A voice from the phone replied.

"My husband, he's been shot in the chest. Please hurry, I don't know how much time he has left," Hannah yelled frantically.

"Triangulating your position. An ambulance is on its way," the voice said.

"Thank you," Hannah said as she hung up.

The rest of the crew started to trickle down the stairs and come out when they heard a shot.

"Jackson, get a sheet from the bedroom quick!" Hannah screamed with tears in her eyes.

"Oh my God, right away," Jackson said.

"What happened?" Rosette asked.

"I don't know, I left him downstairs for a minute to finish his joint, and, when I heard the noise, I turned around and ran back down," Hannah said as she was pressing on Graham's chest trying to get his heart to start again.

Jean looked around the area to see if somebody was nearby with a gun. He couldn't see anything, but he did find a used shell casing on the cement about 15 feet away. Just then, Jackson came down with a sheet.

"Alright. we have to put him on this. Jean, grab his arms and I'll get the feet," Jackson said.

"Alright, on the count of three. THREE!" Jean said.

They picked Graham up and placed him on the sheet. Blood was still coming out of him. Hannah was keeping compression on his chest which was slowing the blood flow down a bit, and she had been able to restart his heart. Everyone just stared at him in disbelief. Not only that he was shot, but that the shot was center mass, and he was still alive. This bullet should have ripped through his heart and killed him instantly. It was a miracle he was still alive.

"Jackson, I found this about 15 feet away," Jean said as he handed him the shell casing.

"Right there?" Jackson asked.

"Exactly," Jean replied.

Jackson turned to everyone, "I'm going after this guy, the ambulance should be here in any minute," Jackson said as he took off before anyone could say anything to him.

Just as Jackson turned the corner, the ambulance came roaring up along the curb.

"OK what do we have here?" The man said as he stepped out of the cabin.

"My husband, he's been shot in the chest!" Hannah screamed.

"OK, we're here now. We'll take good care of him," the man said as he walked up to see what happened. His eyes grew wide, and he went back to the cabin and another man lowered a stretcher onto the ground. They wheeled it up to Graham.

"OK Louis, you got this right? On the count of three we're going to lift him. One, two, THREE!" The man said.

In unison, they lifted Grahams helpless body onto the gurney and wheeled it back to the ambulance.

"On three Louis," the man said.

"You got it Patrick," Louis replied.

On the count of three they lifted it into the ambulance. Just as they were about to close the door Hannah ran up to them.

"I'm coming with you," Hannah demanded.

"That's fine, but only you," Patrick said.

She climbed into the cabin, and they shut the doors from the inside. The driver took off down the street the sirens blaring.

"What is your name?" Louis asked Hannah.

"Hannah, Hannah Newsdon. This is my husband Graham," she replied.

"Wait, are you telling me that this is Graham Newsdon?" Patrick asked.

Hannah nodded her head.

The religious idea of God cannot do full duty for the metaphysical infinity. —Alan Watts

Chapter Two

"Alright everyone, I'm going to do this one time only so listen up," Patrick began, "I got a 28 mm single gunshot, left chest entrance through chest, exit off left armpit. Found him in cardiac arrest, started CPR, decompressed the chest, got a heart rhythm back. Remains unresponsive throughout. Left lung collapse, left pneumothorax breathing was initially labored, trachea was deviated to the right side. Decompressed the left chest, got air escape from the needle. Decompressed the chest, didn't do much. Respiratory response increased; trachea moved back to the midline. O2 sat went from 75 to 85, remains unconscious, respiration rate was 36 before being tubed, heart rate 140. Blood pressure now 76 over 58. Intubated with an 8.5 mm et tube set at 23 centimeters under direct visualization. Capnography has been good throughout. He's got a 16 in each AC," Patrick finished.

"Any other trauma?" A doctor asked.

"No," Patrick replied.

"Family notified?" The same doctor asked.

"Family here," Patrick said as he pointed to Hannah.

"I'm his wife," Hannah replied shaking.

"I'm Dr. Griffin. What is your name?" He asked.

"Hannah," she replied.

"I have to go scrub in. Shoot an X Ray, put the chest tube in to start blood flow. 10 units of 0-. Then bring him directly to OR 1," Dr. Griffin replied.

"Where are we?" Hannah asked still in a daze.

"You're at Brigham and Women's. You're in the best place for cardiac care; don't worry, we have a good team here. You'll have to wait in the waiting room," Dr. Griffin said.

"One more thing doc," Patrick interjected.

"What's that?" He asked.

"This is Graham Newsdon," Patrick said.

"The Graham Newsdon?" Dr. Griffin asked.

Patrick nodded his head.

The room cleared out just as quickly as it packed in. Hannah walked herself back slowly to the waiting room. She was drenched in her husband's blood, and her hands couldn't stop shaking. She took a seat in the far corner by the AC even though she was freezing because nobody was around her. She curled up into a little ball on the chair and started sobbing. The adrenaline was starting to wear off, and she was beginning to get a pounding headache. She texted Rosette and told her where she was. Rosette said they would be on their way. When someone is dying, they say that their life flashes before their eyes; but what they neglect to ever tell you is that when you're significant other is in critical care, YOURS and THEIR life together flash before your eyes. The more Hannah thought about all the happy moments in their life together and on this insane rollercoaster ride that they had been on together the last nearly 10 years, she started to cry more. It was inconceivable to her that she would have to go at it alone now, let alone raise their son alone. Still, it was all up in the air right now. Rosette had texted her and told her that Jean was unsuccessful in finding the man who shot Graham, but that it wasn't over. They had the bullet casing, and that had to be worth something. Rosette told Hannah how they called Wolfgang the cop and gave it to him, and he would look into it. He was also giving them a police escort ride to B&W Hospital. Hannah stood up and got herself a glass of water from the water cooler and pounded it. Then she went up to the desk and asked for a pair of scrubs and a Tylenol. They normally wouldn't have granted that request, but word had started making its rounds that Graham Newsdon and his wife were here. They were in the very best hands, but was that going to be enough?

No one is more hated than he who speaks the truth.
—Plato

Throughout known history, truth has never been popular. It's been kept secret by authority, censored, convoluted, and demonized. Its speakers mocked imprisoned, crucified, assassinated, degraded and suppressed. If your belief system is popular, it cannot be truth. —Gavin Naseimento

Chapter Three

"Dr. Griffin, airway, breathing and circulation are intact. Oxygen Saturation is 97," Dr. Duval said.

"Good. Let's get that chest tube placed. Where is that chest X-ray?" Dr. Griffin asked.

"Vitals please. So this is Graham Newsdon," Dr. Duval said candidly, "Always on a full moon."

"BP 130 over 88, pulse 90, RR 16, temp 97.1, Radiology is on their way," another doctor advised.

"Exit wound left axilla. I wonder why that is?" Dr. Griffin replied.

"Why what is?" Dr. Duval asked.

"Why it's crazy busy on a full moon," Dr. Griffin said as he looked at Grahams chest. How is this guy still alive? Gunshot wound just left of the sternum should have punctured his left ventricle, the main chamber of the heart, the Doctor thought to himself.

"Dr. Griffin, sir, BP is 126 over 78, HR 98 RR 16 O2 Sat 98," Dr. Duval said.

"Give him an additional 500cc bolus stat," Dr. Griffin said.

"I think it's the effect of the moons tidal forces putting pressure on our brains," Dr. Duval said as he administered the bolus.

"That, or extra electromagnetic energy from the center of the galaxy. Let's see that x-ray. Hmmmm…Interesting," Dr. Griffin said.

"Sir, blood pressure is dropping. BP 110 over 70 HR 103 RR 18 O2 is down to 91%!" Dr. Duval enthused.

Dr. Griffin stopped what he was doing and scanned the body. "Look right there. Look at his neck. Distended veins," he said as he was listening to Graham's heart. "Elevate his legs. Bring over the ultrasound machine and let's get another ECG. Prep for pericardiocentesis and make sure the surgeon's on standby," Dr. Griffin said.

"Think of it as galactic electroconvulsive therapy. The full moon acts like a switch in a cosmic circuit. Your brain is the light bulb," Dr. Duval said.

"Interesting. You learn that through our friend Graham's work here?" Dr. Griffin asked as he was prepping the body with iodine.

"Sir, I can't get a pulse or blood pressure," Dr. Duval said.

"Shit! Start CPR," Dr. Griffin said as he cleared the instruments out and Dr. Duval began compressions.

Dr. Duval and Dr. Griffin went back and forth doing compressions for 90 seconds until finally Dr. Griffin spoke up.

"No, we've got to remove the fluid around his heart. His heart can't fill. Give him 1mg Epinephrine IV, let's see if that helps his BP," Dr. Griffin said.

Dr. Duval administered the Epinephrine and they waited. five minutes had gone by.

"Ah, look at that. 70cc of bright red blood," Dr. Duval said holding up a syringe.

"All it takes is 50cc in the pericardial sac to constrict the heart," Dr Griffin said.

"BP is 92 over 60, pulse 90 . . . 120 over 70," Dr. Duval advised. "Shit, he's moving."

"Sorry about that," the Anesthesiologist said as he fixed the situation.

"Clamp!" Dr. Griffin yelped.

"Suction, before his chest cavity fills up with blood," Dr. Duval advised as he sucked up all the extra blood. "It's all different frequencies of energy. The stars and the planets each emit a unique frequency. When they line up, the energies mix and amplify which in turn interacts with our auras which affects our physiology. That's why the lunatics come out during a full moon."

"I'd ligate that vessel first," Dr. Griffin advised.

"Boy, our friend Graham here is going to have some nice scars for the rest of his life," Dr. Duval said. "That was a lot closer than I'd care to have been with him."

2 hours later

"Can I have a straight suture scissor and 2-0 Nylon?" Dr. Griffin asked.

"OK, one more suture and we're out of here," Dr. Duval advised.

"Does the ICU have a bed yet?" Dr. Griffin asked.

"Checking on it right now, we should be good," Dr. Duval said.

The two doctors left the team that was working with them and went into the scrubbing area and took off their masks and gloves.

"I could sure go for a cigarette right about now," Dr. Griffin said.

"You were literally holding Graham Newsdon's heart, and you're talking about smoking?" Dr. Duval asked shocked.

"One of the great mysteries of the world. Why do cardiologists and pulmanologists smoke? Why do psychiatrists have such tumultuous lives? Why are some couples' therapists divorced three times? There's no rhyme or reason to it; it boils down to the individual. Now if you'll excuse me, I need to go out and talk to our friend Graham's wife out there. You're welcome to tag along," Dr. Griffin optioned.

"I'm going to make sure he gets to his ICU bed and stay here just in case something happens. You go ahead. Thank you," Dr. Duval advised.

As Dr. Griffin was making his way to Graham's wife, Hannah, he kept thinking to himself how impressed he was that he could distance himself from the celebrity, if only local, of Graham while he was operating on him. He was also about to give his wife the best news she's heard all day.

Every author in some way portrays himself in his works, even if it be against his will.

—*Johann Wolfgang von Goethe*

Chapter Four

48 hours later

I woke up horrified and scared. One minute I was breathing slowly on the grass in front of our house, the next minute I'm awake with the worst chest pain in my life in a hospital bed. I turned to my right and grabbed the morphine button and pressed it as hard as I could. I assessed my situation. I looked down at my chest and there was a nice set of stitches running down my chest. I turned to my left and saw Hannah there. I called out to her, but she was sleeping, sitting up with her head down. I turned to my right and saw a bunch of nurses in the hallway all sleeping standing up with their heads down. This was beyond creepy. I called out, but nobody could hear me it seemed. I looked down at my chest again and a little further down and noticed a silver string coming out of my belly button. I tugged on it; it became tight. I released it.

"I wouldn't pull too hard on that if I were you. If you snap it, you won't be able to come back," a voice said in the corner of the room.

"What?" I asked as I sat up.

"The string. It's keeping your soul tethered to your body. Look behind you," the man said.

I turned around and saw that my body was still lying down in the bed. I was sitting up directly on it. I jumped up out of fear and looked down. Sure as shit, the silver string was going from belly button to belly button.

"Who are you?" I asked.

The man, who was in the shadows took a few steps towards me. As light began to creep onto his face, I recognized it immediately. I started to choke up.

"Dad?" I asked.

The man took his hat off and revealed himself as my father. He looked identical to the day that he died.

"Hello son," my father replied.

"I don't understand dad. Am I dreaming?" I asked.

"You're in between worlds right now Graham. You survived the surgery, but your body and mind still need to fight to come back," he said.

I looked around and assessed my situation. Everybody was 'asleep'; the only person I could converse with was my father.

"Are you truly my father?" I asked.

14

The man took a deep breath. "Graham, I am, but I've come to you as you remember to make this process easier for you. This is not what I look like right now in reality," he replied.

As I looked at him, I noticed in the corner of my eye a white butterfly land on the windowsill, and then it fluttered towards me. I caught it in my hand and let it sit there and flap its wings.

"The white butterfly is a symbol of new beginnings, sign of future happiness, symbolizes fertility, purity and optimism, good fortunes, peace and serenity, hope and joy. These sort of things. I did not know this would come to you, but it's a very good sign," my father replied.

"Am I in a coma? Am I astral projecting? I see the silver cord," I said.

"You are in between realms. You have a decision to make whether to go back or to stay. If you go back however, you have to finish your work on Earth," he said.

"What is my work on Earth?" I asked.

My father took a minute, took off his overcoat. And then his suit jacket. He rolled up his sleeves and looked to the ceiling and closed his eyes. After about 30 seconds he started to glow the most beautiful white I've ever seen. It was not from this dimension; it was more than just light. It was purely loving, warm. It reminded me of my mother when I was young.

"This is what waits for you if you decide not to go back Graham. It is a higher vibration than you can ever imagine. See, consciousness isn't a place in our brains son. Every cell dies and is replaced. Every 7 years we get an entirely new body. The brain replaces itself every 2 months, yet you experience the same feelings of anxiety, depression, joy, sexual energy, memories. You are not a body with consciousness, you are consciousness with a body. Your five senses become magnified and magnificent in the next dimension," he said.

"The next dimension?" I asked.

"Your soul still grows, and you still have lessons to learn. Depending on what you learn, believe, and figure out on Earth, you will be sent to a new location so to speak where you will continue to learn with souls at your level. You've done quite a bit of discovering all the Astrological connections on Earth as in the Bible. You've saved countless people from fear of a non-existent hell, and also saved people quite literally. But your work is not done. You thought that you destroyed the financial system on Earth and reset it for the greater good, but there is still evil lurking on it, limping along because you haven't cut the head off the snake yet. You need to make a decision whether or not to continue that, or come with me and move along," he said.

I stood up and started pacing around the room.

"Won't I miss Hannah? My son? My friends?" I asked.

"Absolutely, but the grief would be theirs to handle. Where you're going there is no room for pain and suffering. That's the challenge given to us on Earth. You can love them and know that in a short while you can see them again. Remember, time doesn't work the same way as it does on Earth. We're in a multidimensional multiverse with countless realities all at once," he said as he put his jacket back on and stopped glowing.

"What do I have to do when I go back?" I asked.

"That, I can't tell you. Although I've seen into your 'future' I can't tell you because it will impact your free will and that's a law that I'm not allowed to mess with," he said.

I paced around the room taking in everything that was said to me.

"I miss you so much dad," I said.

"Your mother and I miss you too," he replied.

"Mom's with you?" I asked.

"In a sense. She has her own work she has to do; but we are still connected. I'm sorry but I just can't explain to you how it all works until you rip that cord in half and come with me," he replied.

I looked at the cord and held it in my hand. It felt like a celestial rubber band. I know it wouldn't take too much effort to rip it. I thought back to all my friends and what he just said to me and put the cord down.

"I want to go back and finish what I started a long time ago," I replied.

"Very well son. I'm very proud of you. There's just one thing I have to tell you," he said as he made his way towards me.

"What's that dad?" I asked.

"Unfortunately, you're not going to be able to re-member any of this except the white butterfly," he said.

"What do you mean?" I asked.

"Free will remember?" He asked.

I nodded my head.

"You're light and free right now of constraints. When you go back you will enter a finite body, that has pain. This will feel a lot like withdrawal son," he said as he placed his hands on the silver cord. The cord lit up in that brilliant white color, and he shoved me back down into my body. An overwhelming sense of pain hit me. It was time for me to wake up.

Don't worry about anything at all. You are not here by accident. This form is just a costume for a while. But the one who is behind the costume, that one is eternal. You must know this. If you know this and trust this, you don't have to worry about anything. —Mooji

Chapter Five

"HOLY SHIT it hurts!" I screamed waking up.

I scanned the room trying to figure out where I was. Apparently, I'm in the hospital. God damn, my chest fucking hurts. I was having a little trouble taking some deep breaths due to the pain. I turned to my right and saw a bunch of nurses busying themselves. I reached next to me and grabbed the morphine button and pressed it five times as hard as I could.

"Baby, you're awake!" Hannah said.

I turned to her and could tell she had been crying for a bit before I came to. The last thing I remembered was talking to that gentleman from the lecture and then it went dark until I just woke up. Just then the morphine started to kick in. A nurse noticed me and ran off to the nurses' station where a doctor was writing some things down on a chart. She talked to him for a minute; he turned and looked to me. He grabbed another chart, mine I'm assuming, and made his way to me.

"I'm so happy to see you back sweetie," Hannah said.

"What happened?" I asked.

"You were shot Mr. Newsdon. I saved your life," the doctor advised. "You are one of the luckiest people I've ever met."

"Shot?" I asked. Suddenly the pain in my chest made sense.

"Yes sir. How's the pain on a scale of one to ten?" He asked.

"9," I replied.

"That's typical. The morphine should be kicking in shortly. We get alerted when people press the button," he replied.

"Who are you?" I asked.

"I'm Dr. Griffin. We're going to have to keep you a little longer for observation. Boy you're one lucky son of a bitch," he replied.

I was taken aback by his candor.

"I don't understand," I replied.

"You should be dead," Dr. Griffin replied.

"I feel that way," I said as I looked down at my chest. My belly button started to itch. "Doc, if I was shot, why didn't the bullet go through my heart?" I asked.

"You're right, it should have. But lucky for you in this case, you have situs inversus," Dr. Griffin advised.

"What?" I asked.

"Situs Inversus is when the organs are mirror flipped from where they should be. It's a transcription problem within DNA during gestation," he began.

"I know what Situs Inversus is," I said.

"That's right you do," he said looking at my chart. "You were going to be a doctor at one point?" He asked.

"Life has a way of getting in the way of plans," I replied.

"Indeed, I want you to rest for a little while longer and then we'll discharge you. You won't be able to exercise or do any heavy lifting for a bit, but other than that you should be fine," he said.

Situs Inversus? What are the chances. If I had a normal heart, the bullet would have ripped through the walls of the left ventricle, but it was on the other side of my heart. I thought back to all those times when I would get what I thought were spleen pain when I would drink and think it was stones as they would flare up and go away. Now I know that it was my liver telling me to chill the fuck out.

"I'll check back in on you in a couple of hours," Dr. Griffin said as he turned around and left the room.

I turned back to Hannah and smiled. God knows she had been sitting in that seat since I got here.

"How long?" I asked.

"72 hours," she replied.

That shook me a bit. It literally felt like one second I was in front of my house, and the split next second I was in the hospital. But three days had passed. I thought back to the story of how the Sun remains dead for three days and then comes back to life. Was I writing my own hero's journey?

"Baby, you'll be happy to know that we caught the guy that shot you," Hannah said.

"How?" I asked.

"We found the slug from the gun, and we were able to match a fingerprint. He lived a few towns over. Officer Wolfgang picked him up yesterday morning," she said.

"Well, that's good. Why?" I began.

"Why did he shoot you? He was a radicalized religious nut who was at your lecture at the TD Bank Arena. He went there with the intention of shooting you. You actually had a conversation with him during the lecture," she said.

"I did?" I asked.

"Try and relax sweetie. Eventually things will come back to you," she said.

I was about to close my eyes when she nudged me.

"You're going to want to see these first before you go back to bed," Hannah said.

I looked as she turned around and picked up a few local newspapers. I grabbed them and sat up. All of them had articles about how I had been shot. One of them even said that I was dead.

"I guess I'm going to have to sue someone aren't I?" I asked.

"What's the point, don't let it get to you," she replied.

"How is everyone else?" I asked.

"At the house. A nervous wreck. But better since I just texted Rosette while Dr. Griffin was talking to you," she said.

I stretched out and looked up at the ceiling. The lights were a little softer, but I knew that was the effect of the morphine.

"I already have your pain medication baby, I filled it up from the pharmacy downstairs a little while ago. Truth is we were waiting for you to wake up any hour," Hannah replied.

"I'm starving, can I get something to eat?" I asked.

"You know how this works. Ice chips for now," she said as she handed me a cup of ice pellets.

I had this feeling brewing inside me that something was missing or that I wasn't being told everything.

"How's James?" I asked.

"Oh, he's fine. We made something for you," Hannah said as she went into her purse and pulled it out. I felt her place it in my hands.

"Open your eyes. James was very proud of this," she said.

I opened my eyes and looked down into my hands. It was an origami of a white butterfly. I sat up. I remember something about a butterfly but couldn't quite get to it. Almost as if I was trying to remember someone else's dream would be the best way I could describe it.

"It's beautiful," I said.

"It was all his idea. He said it would bring you good luck, when we get out of here, we'll go see him. The crew is with him at home right now. He has no idea you've been shot, only that you have a boo boo," Hannah said.

A tear crept into my eye and fell down on my face.

"Get some rest Graham. We'll be out of here soon enough," Hannah advised.

I closed my eyes. The morphine indeed kicked in, but I slowed my breathing down even more which helps me fall asleep. Though my eyes were closed, I could see red through my eyelids due to the lights above. As I drifted back asleep, the last thing I saw amongst the red was that little white butterfly.

The biggest thing you need to understand is that God/Consciousness whatever you want to call it is infinite even beyond our dimension. Nothing exists outside the infinite, and we are all a small part of the all experiencing itself subjectively in this illusionary place called earth where real things are made up of things that cannot be regarded as real as Bohr said 100 years ago when quantum physics was first birthed. Thinking we are separate from God and creating that division between us as a deity that must be worshipped is literally where all the problems come from in the world. It's the epicenter of it all. The good, the bad, the everything is what we experience in this dimension. Isaiah 45:7 explains briefly why there is good and bad in the world. We are all God. This isn't new age, this goes back thousands of years before the Bible. —MD

Chapter Six

Mount Snow, Vermont
4 months later (March 17th)

We got to our rented house on Snowfall Lane and met Filthy at the door. His name was Richard, but we all called him filthy. We unpacked our suitcases into the drawers and took up our rooms.

"Alright guys, who's going skiing today?" He asked.

"No skiing, we're doing the innertube today aren't we buddy?" I said as I turned and asked James.

"Yay daddy yay!" He replied.

"I'm going to go into the hot tub with Rosette and Larisa for a little bit," Hannah said to me.

"OK, we got up here earlier than I thought, so we have an hour or two," I replied.

"Did everyone bring their costumes?" Larisa asked as she dragged her suitcase through the door.

"Jean, what are you doing? Help her," Jackson said.

Jean was lugging two suitcases and his hands were full. "Mon ami, I'm already dealing with two of hers!" he said.

Jackson laughed as he grabbed the suitcase from Larisa and brought it into their room.

"Hey Graham, can I get you and James something to drink?" Filthy asked.

"I'll take a seltzer. James, what do you want? Do you want some juice?" I asked.

"Apple juice," James replied.

"Sure, I've got some left, hold on," Filthy said as he walked to his refrigerator. He took out a can for me and poured a glass of apple juice for James.

"Filthy, are you coming in the hot tub with us?" Rosette asked.

"I thought you'd never ask," Filthy replied as he took his shirt off and ripped off his track pants. The girls giggled.

"How does that gold chain of yours not get stuck in your bright white nipple hair?" Jackson asked as he came out of the room.

"You're just jealous you don't have this look," Filthy replied. "Although, I'd kill to look like you Jax."

Jackson laughed.

"What are we going to do in the meantime?" Jean asked.

"There's rock band set up downstairs if you want to play with James," Filthy said as he put on tanning lotion.

"It's 25 degrees outside. Why are you putting on tanning lotion?" I asked.

"I burn easily," Filthy replied.

"We wouldn't want you to look like a hairy dog penis now, would we?" Jackson asked.

"One day Jax, I hope you're able to ride like I do at my age," Filthy said as he started gyrating.

"OK, I have a child here Filthy, knock it off," Hannah replied.

"Sorry," Filthy said.

28

"Filthy, did you know that 96% of the US population has oxybenzone in their bodies which is a known endocrine disrupter that is linked to reduced sperm count in men and endometriosis in women. The main source is sunscreen," I said.

"I guess my older brothers high school graduation song "Everybody loves Sunscreen" by Baz Luhrman was a psy op then?" Jackson asked.

The girls got in the hot tub. I brought them a few beers and set them in the snow to keep them cold for them. Filthy brought his ale horn with him. Honestly, this guy is like a cartoon. We went downstairs and played rock band for an hour until James started to get sleepy. Before long he was passed out on the couch behind him. I brought him upstairs and put him in the bed in our room. I got the girls towels from the closet in the bathroom and brought Filthy his white robe. They dried off and Filthy lit a cigar. Honestly, looking at him in a white robe with his white chest hair poking out smoking a cigar and you could tell he was the King of Vermont.

"Hey Graham, I've got a little bit of weed left over in the joint in the ashtray if you want it," Filthy said.

I turned and looked over to Hannah. She shrugged her shoulders. Fuck it, we were on vacation, my first real trip since that incident went down a few months ago. My chest finally felt back to normal. I went into the living room and lit it up. I took a few baby drags off it, not trying to cough my lungs out. Too late. I started coughing up a storm. When you cough it actually gets you more higher for a couple of reasons. It's funny because growing up when I used to smoke in my early teens, I would get such anxiety and paranoia. Though I was drinking at the time as well so it would make me very dizzy, and I'd end up throwing up sometimes. But since I quit drinking and my anxiety and depression had gone away, and I had been properly medicated, the only thing that happened to me was that it relaxed me. It was like taking a Xanax without the sleepiness.

"Alright guys, are we ready to go to Cuzzins or what?" Rosette asked.

Cuzzins was a local place in Mount Snow that was throwing a killer St. Patricks day parade. I nodded and stood up and cocked my head to the bedroom to indicate people to follow me to get changed. After a few minutes, we all came out looking Irish as ever for this event. All except Hannah.

"Hey babe, I'm going to stay here with James. I want to be here when he wakes up. Plus, I want to make sure that Filthy doesn't eat him," Hannah said.

"I heard that!" Filthy replied.

Rosette and Larisa giggled.

"All right. I'll drop you all off and come home and order us some takeout. I need to take a nap anyway," Filthy answered.

"Old man," Jackson said.

"Shut it brute squad," Filthy replied.

We all packed into Filthys Escalade and made our way to Cuzzins. It wasn't very far. It was just as I remembered it.

"Alright guys, I'll be back in a few hours to get you. Keep your phones on vibrate because it's loud in there and I'll text you when I'm on my way," Filthy said.

"Thanks bud," I replied.

We made our way into the barn/hotspot. It was going to be a great time. Great friends, nice party. Little did we know that there would be news to shock the nation.

What if biblical prophecies are coming true because the same elites that wrote the Bible are still controlling the world today? —Anonymous

Chapter Seven

We pulled up to Cuzzins and got out.

"Alright, I'll see you guys in 3-4 hours. Try not to get lost," Filthy said.

"Thanks for the ride," I said as I closed the door.

We walked in and it was a wild time. The entire place was decorated for St. Patrick's Day; we all walked up to the bar and got some drinks. I turned around with my diet coke and led everybody to a table near the front where we could sit.

"How are you feeling Graham, mon ami?" Jean asked referring to my smoking just before.

"You know Jean, I was wondering. Do French people smoke weed, or do they smoke oui'd?" I asked.

Rosette laughed.

"By the way, Feliz CUMpleanos to you Jackson. Happy birthday my brother," I shouted.

"Hey, Penis Navidad, Happy new rear to you!" he replied.

"You know, I always wanted to go to a Tony Robbins seminar high on mushrooms. Would you come with me?" I asked him.

"I don't think I could handle such an amazing time. I think my small penis would shrivel up and fall off," he said.

"What do you mean small? Dude you're like 6'7". There's no way," Larisa said to him.

"You know you'd think that, but I'm a grower not a shower. You ever snip the head off a fat Cuban cigar?" He asked.

"You're the cigar?" Larisa asked.

"No, I'm the fat head that clipped off," Jackson said as he took a sip of his mixed drink.

"That's weird because I know for a fact that Rosette likes it doggie style. She likes it ruff, ruff, ruff," Larisa said as she winked to Rosette.

Rosette giggled.

"That's not all the conspiracy girl likes," Jackson laughed.

"Oh, so you brown pilled her then?" I asked.

Rosette turned bright red.

"The key to it is that you have to relax your asshole chakra," Larisa said.

"What about you Graham?" Rosette asked as she started to turn back to normal color.

"I'm going to start a go fuck me request online. It's hard with kids you know," I replied.

"Sure, I'll donate to a go fuck yourself request," Jackson replied.

I laughed. "Don't be a douchekabob."

"You know guys, the stethoscope was invented because a male doctor felt uncomfortable with putting his ear to a womans naked breast. That's chivalry. You assholes make anal jokes about me," Rosette replied.

"If the shoe fits," I said.

"Careful Graham," Jackson said as he took a huge gulp of his drink, "Say it again and I'll drag you into Tiger Schulmanns and then beat your ass," he finished.

"Yeah, def don't want that," I replied as I finished my diet coke and went back to the bar for another one.

I made my way back to everyone and saw they were having a great time.

"You know if I were a woman, you'd have 25 kids by now Jax," I said.

"No, you wouldn't. I've been drinking pineapple juice all month," he said as he winked at me.

Rosette spit out some of her drink.

"That's just gross Jackson," Larisa said.

"Oh, I see, ok so THAT's where we draw the line. Got it," he replied.

"You know I always wondered about you two," Jean said.

"Like my French friend Jean over here, there was a playwright and French novelist named Honore de Balzac. Larisa, do you Honore de Balzac?" I asked.

Larisa turned red. What is it with these two girls not being able to keep up.

"Your wife would have stoned you by now for the way you're talking to us," Larisa advised.

"Oh please. My kid's asleep and she's back there taking her Osteo Buttflex and doing squats," I said.

"Is that another anal joke? Because I can't take much more of this," Rosette advised.

"Is that right Hairy Potter? Don't worry, if you're too sore, when we get back to the house, I'll cook us all up some Nyquil chicken so we can sleep through the 'pain'," I said laughing.

"You really missed a golden chance. Instead of your book series called Into the Rabbit Hole, it should have been into the booty hole," Jean said.

We all stopped and looked at Jean.

"Why would you say such a thing?" Jackson asked.

"Yeah Jean, that was just mean," I replied.

"Are you guys serious?" He asked looking nervous.

We kept our cool for about 15 seconds until we burst out laughing.

"You know the female world record for the most or-gasms in an hour is 134 while the males is 16," Rosette said, finally back to her natural color.

"I'd be passed out by 2. Also, I shoot disappearing and reappearing ink," I said.

"I could hit 10-15 before I probably shit the bed," Larisa advised as she sneezed and let a fart slip out.

"Perfect timing," I said.

"Yeah Larisa, you play trumpet for MIT's band?" Rosette asked.

"Yo, for real, you got a tight little butthole, don't you?" I asked laughingly.

"Ok guys, I get it. Ha ha. Very funny," Larisa said.

"No seriously, I'd totally pay you for your farts in a jar though," Jackson said.

I burst out laughing.

We all made our way to the bar to get another round of drinks. When we turned around, we were faced with some familiar faces that we hadn't seen since middle school.

"Hey there Graham. Where's your wife?" Alyssa asked.

"Yeah Graham, who are your friends? Are any of them single? Stephanie asked.

"I have to pee," Angella said as she turned to run to the bathroom.

"What the hell are you girls doing up in Mount Snow?" I asked.

"Duh, we have a winter house up here. I heard you're staying with Filthy. How's that guy doing?" She asked.

"You know, has his two dogs watching porn all the time. He went in the hot tub with us greased up like a turkey in the oven with sun block," Rosette said.

"That's hysterical," Steph said.

"So really, what are you doing at Cuzzins today?" I asked.

"Well, it's kind of Alyssa's fault," Steph said.

"What do you mean?" I asked.

"So, we lent out one of the mountain passes, and it got confiscated because it wasn't the right person. So, we're here giving out lap dances for cash to make back the 1500 dollars for the pass," Alyssa said.

"Well, how much have you made back so far?" Jackson asked.

"2300," Angella answered as she got back.

"Shit, well, keep at it," I said.

"Do you want to dance for some cash big boy?" Steph asked Jackson.

"No thanks, I'm here for a good time not a long time," Jackson said.

"Suit yourself. This your man?" Steph asked Rosette.

"Yes, Steph. His name is Jackson. We met in grad school," Rosette said.

"Well good for you girl!" Steph advised.

"Alright ladies, we have to go back to the grind. The booze tonight isn't going to pay for itself," Alyssa said.

"See you guys later maybe?" Steph asked.

"Maybe, we'll be here for a little longer," I said.

The girls went away, and we were back to our normal bullshit dirty conversation until the DJ cut the music.

"Alright everyone, I'm sorry to put this party on hold, but somethings happening. Turn the volume up on that TV right there," he said.

Everyone was silent as the TV was turned on.

As of 2 hours ago, the President of the United States has suffered a heart attack and slipped into a coma. All is being done to revive him and bring him back to us. In the meantime, Vice President Josh Bedpine has been sworn in as President. In his first act as acting President, he has reneged the committee to search for a better financial situation that has been the former President's crux. This is a breaking story, and we will continue to bring live updates as

soon as we have them. In the meantime, this is Jennifer Polizzi signing out for AquaNews.

We sat there stunned at the news. What a total buzzkill from this party. I went to my phone and texted Filthy to come pick us up when I noticed an email unread in my phone. Thinking nothing of it I clicked on it.

Graham,

You don't know me, but I am a close adviser to President Rand Dotplum. He has always thought of you in the highest regard for many years. I don't know who to trust or who to turn to here, but I fear he might have been poisoned. If you hadn't known before, there was a lot of mixed emotions within the cabinet regarding his wanting to switch over to cryptocurrency and possibly abolish the Federal Reserve. I fear someone in the cabinet may be behind this, but I have no proof yet. All I can tell you is that he left you a message in the event something happened to him and entrusted me to get it. Here it is below, completely unredacted:

Graham, this is President Dotplum. I have been taking the New World Order head on, but I fear that my time may be coming soon. I am getting older, and it may be seen that something natural will happen to me in order to get me out of the way. I have discovered something truly mind blowing, but I can't just come out and share it with you in case this gets intercepted. Just know that 'Liberty is not the torch of Freedom' and you have to put the nail in the coffin.

We hope that you can be of service to us under the radar. Everything is locked down here. I fear the worst. I have accessed your emails through a computer programmer here that I trust. If you need to comment to me, write a draft email, but don't send it, leave it in drafts. Then text 4914118 to 181144. I will check and reach back out to you when I have a reply.

—D

A sick feeling hit the pit of my stomach. This reminded me exactly of how I felt when I got that email from James all those years ago. In my heart I didn't know if I had the wherewithal to go through with something else again, but I also knew equally that they wouldn't have reached out to me unless they were desperate.

"Hey guys, we need to go now," I said.

"Why, what's wrong?" Larisa asked

"It's happening again," I said.

"Quoi?" Jean asked.

"I'll explain when we get back to Filthy's," I said.

We went outside and he was waiting for us. We piled into the car and the entire car ride home was silent.

"Shit, you guys ok?" Filthy asked.

"I don't know yet," I replied.

We got back to Filthy's and settled in. My son had just woken up. I explained everything to Hannah and we agreed that she would stay with James in Vermont until we figured everything out.

"We have to go back home guys, I'm sorry to cut this trip short, but I fear we don't have much time," I said.

We all piled into the van and Jean started the car. It was going to be strange not having Hannah along for this, but at the very least I had to know that my wife and kid was safe while we got thrown into the middle of something we weren't quite sure about. On the way

home I read everybody the email I received, and everyone was silent. We had no idea what we were about to
get ourselves into.

I have examined all the known superstitions of the world, and I do not find in our particular superstition of Christianity one redeeming feature. They are all alike founded on fables and mythology. Millions of innocent men, women, and children, since the introduction of Christianity, have been burnt, tortured, fined and imprisoned. What has been the effect of this coercion? To make one half the world fools and the other half hypocrites; to support roguery and error all over the earth.
— *Thomas Jefferson*

Chapter Eight

"You know Graham, shrooming in your 20's is on pizza. Shrooming as you get to your 30's is on cauliflower pizza," Jackson said laughing.

"Thanks, Jax, but I'm too nervous to laugh right now," I said as we pulled up to my house and walked inside.

We made our way up the stairs and into the living room.

"Alright Larisa, do your thing," I said.

"Roger that," she replied as she opened up my email and put it on the screen in the living room.

Graham,

You don't know me, but I am a close adviser to President Rand Dotplum. He has always thought of you in the highest regard for many years. I don't know who to trust or who to turn to here, but I fear he might have been poisoned. If you hadn't known before, there was a lot of mixed emotions within the cabinet regarding his wanting to switch over to cryptocurrency and possibly abolish the Federal Reserve. I fear someone in the cabinet may be behind this, but I have no proof yet. All I can tell you is that he left you a message in the event something happened to him and entrusted me to get it. Here it is below, completely unredacted:

Graham, this is President Dotplum. I have been taking the New World Order head on, but I fear that my time may be coming soon. I am getting older, and it may be seen that something natural will happen to me in order to get me out of the way. I have discovered something truly mind blowing, but I can't just come out and share it with you in case this gets intercepted. Just know that 'Liberty is not the torch of Freedom' and to put the nail in the coffin.

We hope that you can be of service to us under the radar. Everything is locked down here. I fear the worst. I have accessed your emails through a computer programmer here that I trust. If you need to comment to me, write a draft email, but don't send it, leave it in drafts. Then text 4914118 to 181144. I will check and reach back out to you when I have a reply.

—D

"OK so first of all, who is D?" Rosette asked.

"I have no idea," I replied.

"The Liberty is not the torch of Freedom? What is that supposed to mean?" Jean asked.

"I have no idea," I replied.

"Well, what do we know?" Jackson asked.

"I have no idea!" I shouted.

"Alright everyone, let's just calm down," Rosette said.

I went to the kitchen and grabbed myself a diet snapple. I came back into the living room with a thought.

"Wasn't Blur very close with Rand Dotplum?" I asked.

"They were, before Blur and Rand were both taken off social media. Why do you ask?" Rosette asked.

"I'm going to run this by him and see what he thinks," I said as I flipped open my phone and dialed the number. It rang to voicemail. I hung up. Just then a phone call came in from the same area code. I picked it up and put it on speaker.

"Hello Graham," the voice said.

I recognized the voice as Swey Honorer, his afternoon anchor.

"Blur can't come to the phone, but is there something I might be able to help you out with?" Swey asked.

"I hope so," I said as I read him what the advisor said.

"Call me on the computer so I can see you. Same number," Swey said as he hung up.

I shrugged my shoulders and nodded to Larisa. She dialed from the computer and put the image on the big screen.

"I see you have some friends with you. I recognize them from your book series. How are you doing everyone?" Swey asked.

We all nodded.

"Good," he said. "Graham, you may want to sit down for this, this is going to be a long one," he continued.

I took a seat next to Jackson. I was starting to miss my wife and kid, but we had all agreed this was for the best.

"There was a lot of mixed emotions within the cabinet regarding his wanting to switch over to cryptocurrency and possibly abolish the Federal Reserve. This is the end game Graham," Swey said.

"I don't understand. I thought that we had destroyed the financial institutes," I replied.

"Don't you know that there's always a contingency plan Graham? From all our available intel that's come through to us, the banking empire is still being controlled. Problem is, we have no idea where from," he said.

"What do you mean banking empire?" Rosette asked.

"Banks have done more injury to the religion, morality, tranquility, prosperity, and even wealth of the nation than they can have done or ever will do good. That was John Adams. It is no coincidence that the century of total war coincided with the century of central banking. That was Ron Paul. Everything, and I mean

EVERYTHING, wrong with the world goes back to the banking and more specifically the Schrodhilts," Swey said.

"I don't understand," Larisa advised.

"That's ok. Nobody knows this history, at least the people that do know can't do anything about it. Let's rewind the clock back to the Battle of Waterloo. Amschel Schrodhilt was a banker and a businessman. He founded a firm in London. His firm's money was made by supplying the Duke of Wellington's army in Spain and France with gold and silver coins to pay the troops. But even that wasn't enough for him. What he did was set up a private courier system that would speed relay information on horses and also had some carrier pigeons as well. On June 18th, he sent an agent to Dunkirk. Napoleon was in trouble, and it seemed like his fall was likely. The stock market was set to explode. However, he was in sole possession of this news. When the courier came back and talked to him, Amschel sold off all his assets as people worried that Napoleon had won, began selling them all off, because you see, he had the early intel. Once everybody sold everything off, Amschel Schrodhilt bought back EVERYTHING at pennies on the dollar. When word came back that Napoleon had indeed lost, people started buying again which soared his fortune to an ungodly amount. He has been on record saying that it was the best piece of business he had ever done. Fast forward now to America, which had a central bank set up. Alexander Hamilton was the first head of it; he was killed in a duel. They put his face on the ten dollar bill. They attempted to set up another central bank and when Andrew Jackson was President he put all his might into fighting it off. He survived several assassination attempts on his life. Finally, he did pay the debt back to the bank and on his death bed his final words were "I killed the banks," which in the future they put his face on the twenty dollar bill. Fast forward now to Lincoln who had another central bank to deal with. He decided that he wanted the United States to print and charter its own money instead of the central bank. He was about to issue what were called 'greenbacks' which were dollars that were redeemable with gold. Right before it took place, he was assassinated. They put him on the penny and the five dollar bill. Now, fast forward to 1912. There was a meeting on Jeckyl Island off Carolina where the heads of all the banking families met. They decided they would create another central bank and call this one the Federal Reserve to confuse people. This was as Federal as Federal Express was, that is to say it wasn't. It also wasn't a reserve. Up until now, the dollars used to be backed by silver or gold. There were a few people that were against it and publicly made statements against it. Jacob Astor, Isidor Straus and Benjamin Guggenheim. All notable men whose names still stand. These people at Jeckyl Island set up a plot to destroy the Titanic, which all 3 men would be on. Once it sunk, they went through with Jeckyl Island. Next, we fast forward to 1913. Woodrow Wilson was the President, and he signed into effect the Federal Reserve Act. Their banking plan had worked. Woodrow Wilson was quoted as saying 'I am a most unhappy man. I have unwittingly ruined my country. A great industrial nation is controlled by its system of credit'. For this they put him on the face of the 100,000 dollar bill. Before 1913, people kept 100% of their paychecks. Yet there were still roads, schools etc. Almost immediately the dollar started to devalue. Fast forward now to 1962. President John F. Kennedy snuck into the White House. He was the first Catholic and non WASP President and that was because their family used all the bootleg liquor money to hoist him there. He also famously was on TV debating Richard Nixon, and he noticed that there was a shadow over Richard's face, by the way he composed himself. Noticing this, Kennedy held his face up higher, thus avoiding the shadow. In black and white TV, it looked very much like an evil man verses a younger good looking man. Kennedy set forth an executive order 11110, which was set to abolish the Federal Reserve and have the United States print their own money. On November 22nd, the handover date from Scorpio (the betrayer) to Sagittarius (the death) he was assassinated. The first thing Lyndon Johnson did when he took over as President was rescind that executive order. They rewarded Kennedy by putting him on the 50 cent coin. Money is the root of all evil. It seems that anybody that fights the central banks ends up losing their lives, then memorialized on money as a sort of eternal fuck you to them. This is around the time that Frecklerole became the CEO of Chase Bank. Now, it's important to know that silver to gold ration has typically since the 14th CENTURY traded at 13 to 1. When he became CEO, the values became manipulated. There was even a half assed investigation into it. With gold and silver being so unstable, people kept with this useless paper money. Before the Federal Reserve, a dollar used to say redeemable for Gold. Now after it, it said, This note is legal tender for all debts, public and private. See here's the thing. Money is printed out of thin air and with interest. If I print 1000 dollars for you and charge you 5% interest, you can NEVER pay it off because where is the money coming to pay the interest? So, you have to take out more money. It's a ponzi scheme that has devalued the dollar 99% since the Federal Reserve's inception. Fast forward to the 70's. Richard Nixon winning the

Presidency eventually makes everyone use the American dollar as the global oil trade. He also removes the backing of it by gold. The world uses American dollars for oil, which are backed by nothing now. There are only a handful of countries that do not have the Schrodhilt central banks in them. When Libya got toppled, the FIRST thing they did was install a central bank. All the countries that do not have central banks, the media paint to be evil and sway people's minds on them. Recently the Russians had paid back their debt and kicked out the Schrodhilts and you see what's going on in Russia now and in what the mainstream media is saying. These are the people that OWN the corporations, that OWN the corporations, that OWN the media. If you default on your debt, they manufacture stories in the news that push the public to want war. As summed up perfectly by the matriarch of the Schrodhilt family, Gutle Schnaper, "If my sons did not want wars, there would be none." THIS is the root of everything that's evil. That's why most of the world is broke and people live in abject poverty. This is why there are wars, why militaries are built up. War is very profitable, peace is not. Many of the elites finance both sides of every war in order to make money. Now, with all that being said, Liberty is not the torch of freedom is very poignant. This makes me think of the Statue of Liberty. See, Liberty is not freedom.

Liberty is what sailors get when they come to shore for a short time. It all goes back to maritime law which is the ruling law of the World. There are rumors that there is a trail that leads to the head of it all. The head of the financial world. Before the Schrodhilt's went underground recently and were buried alive in their city caves, they set up a path to be led to the one. In case a catastrophe happens. Which incidentally, in the IRS's handbook, there is a section that talks about how to collect taxes if a Nuclear War happens a month after. This will never stop, and we can never heal the world until we get rid of these people. The torch, there are two torches at the Statue of Liberty, which incidentally is the pagan goddess Semiramis, the whore of Babylon, a homewrecker and harlot. She represents the destruction of the Old World Order and the creation of the New World Order. There must be a clue there, Graham. Finally, although the Roman Empire allegedly fell 1700 years ago despite never being defeated militarily, a total of 142 Greco-Roman triumphal monuments have been identified in over 40 countries. For example, the Romans had Capitoline Hill, whereas we have Capitol Hill. Same architecture. Greco Roman columns have been identified in over 177 high profile governmental, legal, monetary and political buildings around the world including Buckingham Palace in London, the National

Capitol in Bogata, the Federal Palace of Switzerland. The Government Conference Center in Ottawa, the Great Hall of the people in Beijing, the Iranian Parliament Building in Tehran, the National Capitol Building in Havana Cuba, the Old Supreme Court Building in Singapore the Reichstag Building in Berlin, The Royal Palace in Oslo, Norway, the White House in America, 42 of 50 US State Capital Buildings, the US Supreme court building and the NY Stock Exchange. A total of 1114 Roman domes have been identified so far, most of which are religious buildings such as basilicas, cathedrals, churches, mosques, and temples. Romans were the first to build the dome. A total of 227 Greco Roman obelisks have been identified around the world thus far such as Cleopatra's Needle in London, The Vatican Piazza, San Pietro Obelisk in Rome, the Washington Monument. Although the Romans have a 13-month calendar, and the Jews have a Hebrew calendar, over 90% of their holy days fall on the same date in the Gregorian Calendar. All 12 Jewish holy days, Hannukah, Hoshanah Rabbah, Passover, Purim, Rosh Hashanah, Shavuot, Shemini Atzeret, Simchat Tora, Tisha B'Av, Tu Bishvat, Yom Kippur and Sukkot all fall on Roman Holy days. The Roman Senate was traditionally founded in 753 BC and is still active. There are 53 active Senates found in the World Today. Rome never fell; it just hid and spread its tentacles into every other country," Swey finished as he took a giant sip of water.

"Jesus Christ, this financial situation has been going on for 300 years?" Larisa asked.

"How do people not know about any of this?" Jackson asked.

"They own the news, they own the banks. These are psychopaths. Centuries of psychopaths that control everything. If you can get to the head of it all, we might have a fighting chance Graham. I have to go now; the Raw Room is coming on soon and I have to host. I'll text you my number. Feel free to reach out," Swey said as he turned the camera off.

We sat there looking at one another. I had known about some of this stuff, like when NP figured out the conspiracy behind who goes on the money, but definitely not into this much detail. One thing was for sure, we had to get to the Statue of Liberty asap. Something told me we don't have a lot of time left.

Russia said it will eliminate the dollar from its National Wealth Fund to reduce vulnerability to Western sanctions just two weeks before the Russian President holds his first summit meeting with US leader Josh Bedpine. Look into what happened to Saddam Hussein in Iraq, Ghaddafi in Libya and Assad in Syria when they tried the same thing. How did things turn out for them?

—MD

Chapter Nine

March 18th

9:30 AM

"We've got to get to the Statue of Liberty," I said as I turned to everyone.

"But how? Even if we get there, there's no way that we'll be able to get to the torch to find what's hidden there," Rosette said.

"We need to go at night," Jean said.

"But even then, we need someone to get us there. I don't have a boat, do you?" Larisa said.

"I have an idea," I said as I pulled out my phone, dialed Hannah and walked into the bedroom.

"Hey baby, how are you doing?" Hannah replied.

"We're fine; we've got to get to the Statue of Liberty. Can you reach out to Dannick and see if he has any connections there?" I asked.

"Oh, Graham. I believe his ex-girlfriend is a Coast Guard. I'll see what I can do," she said as she hung up the phone and walked back in the room.

"She's working on it," I said.

"What we need is the Alcubierre Warp Drive," Jackson said.

"What are you talking about now baby?" Rosette replied.

"It allows us to move faster than the speed of light across space. See, as you accelerate towards the speed of light, your mass becomes infinite, so you'll never reach it. But rather than doing that, a spacecraft would travel the distance by contracting space in front of it and expanding space behind it. It shifts space around an object so that the object would arrive at its destination faster than light would in normal space without breaking any laws of physics," Jackson finished.

"Uh huh, and let me ask you this. How would that be applicable to us on Earth. You're talking about traveling around the Earth in under 3 seconds. Also, how would we not liquify as people?" Rosette asked.

"Well, I haven't gotten that far yet, I mean it's only theoretical," Jackson said.

"How about we talk about things that are practical then," I replied.

"Graham, your work is a perfect example of the 100th Monkey effect," Rosette began.

"What now?" I asked.

"It's when a new behavior or idea is spread rapidly through consciousness, from one group to the rest of the species once a critical number is reached," Rosette said.

"You're talking about my books?" I asked.

"Exactly. I don't know why you stopped writing them. Consciousness is fundamental. I bet you didn't know that the Universe is conscious, and we are all sharing one great consciousness; so when an idea hit's a critical mass, it expands exponentially," Rosette said.

"I know about consciousness being fundamental, that's cutting-edge Quantum Physics," Jackson replied.

"It's actually not, if you read the Emerald Tablets of Thoth or the Quantum Hermetica you'll see that it's a very old idea that's just coming to the surface now," I said.

Just then my phone rang. I was so excited that I flung it out of my hands and across the room. I ran to the couch and picked it up. I had missed a call from an unknown number.

"Good job butterfingers," Jean said.

"Shut up," I said.

I typically don't pick up random numbers because it could be the press, or it could be a fan that got my number somehow. Every time I pick up a random number it never ends well. Just then Hannah called.

"Guys it's Hannah, can you be quiet a minute?" I asked.

"Waiting around here when we have to be in New York is as useless as the comments section in a porn video," Jackson said.

"Excuse me?" Rosette said.

"There are comment sections in sexy videos?" Jean asked.

"Sometimes what I like to do is go on them and write 'Why are you doing this? Your mother and I are heartbroken, please come home,' " Jackson said.

I stared at him. "I fucking can't with you," I said as I went back into the bedroom.

"Hi baby, sorry," I said.

"Did you get a missed call yet?" She asked.

"Well yeah I did, but it was a rando, so I didn't pick up," I replied.

"Ugh, Graham, sweetie, honey, baby, that was Dannick. He's going to meet you in the city. His ex-girlfriend put in for a day transfer to work on a coast guard boat that circles the Statue of Liberty at night, but it has to be tonight or tomorrow, otherwise they will get suspicious. Get to New York," Hannah said.

"How's James, can I talk to him?" I asked.

"Not now he's sleeping," she replied.

"How's Filthy behaving. Am I going to have to kill him?" I asked.

"He's fine, his two dogs are playing with James all day, I barely have to do anything," she said.

"Alright, well thank you for that hun," I said.

"Oh, and Graham," she began.

"Yes?" I asked.

"Call that number back and meet up with him," Hannah said as she hung up.

I put the phone in my pocket and walked back into the living room.

"OK, so we're in. We have to do this today or tomorrow though. Jean, can you ready the plane?" I asked.

"Non, mon ami, it's being serviced," Jean said.

"Shit, OK, so are taking an Amtrak down or getting plane tickets?" Larisa asked.

"I'll use my points. I'll get us the tickets. If I remember correctly, we can fly into JFK, take the shuttle to Jamaica, then hop on a train to Penn Station and meet Dannick there," Rosette said.

"Great, I'll give Dannick a call, and we should all pack light," I said as I pulled my phone out and went to redial the missed call.

I spoke to Dannick, and he agreed to meet us at Penn Station at 5PM. It's still early March in New York and the Sun has not crossed the Equator, daylight savings is not on, so it gets dark earlier. This could be to our advantage. Everybody went home to pack and come back.

After about 90 minutes, everyone was back at my house, ready to go. We piled into the van and made our way to Logan. If we had only known that we had a very specific timeframe that we had to be on, we might have figured things out differently. Also, we were not ready for how wild Dannick's ex-Missy was going to be.

The bankers will ensure we stay in debt. The pharmaceutical companies will ensure we stay sick. The weapons manufacturers will ensure we keep going to war. The media will ensure we are prevented from knowing the truth. The government will ensure all of this is done legally. —Anonymous

Chapter Ten

March 18th

1:30 p.m.

It had been a long time since we sat in a plane that wasn't Jeans. I started to get a panic attack when I saw how small the seats were. Lucky for us, Rosette sprung for first class seats, which instantly made me feel like humping her leg. We put our bags away and sat down. Within 30 minutes we were in the air.

"I hope this didn't break the bank girl," Larisa said to Rosette.

"Don't worry about it, I can always turn Jean upside down and shake some money out of him," she said winking and smiling to Larisa. She then blew her a kiss.

Larisa giggled.

"You two need help," Jean said.

I closed my eyes to try and relax for this very short flight. I was awakened with a tap.

"Hey, you're Graham Newsdon aren't you?" A man across from me said.

I smiled back at him.

"You're not going to shoot me? Are you?" I asked.

"No, no no no of course not. So, I've been following your work. According to Blavatsky's secret doctrine, the first dimension is metals/minerals, the second is plants, the third is animals and the 4th is man. What do you think the next ones are, and do we need to understand the work you've been doing in order to ascend?" He asked.

Usually I wouldn't have engaged in this kind of conversation, especially when my mind was in another place altogether, but he seemed nice and genuinely interested.

"I think that's a question you'd have to ask my friend Jackson here about," I said.

"What's that Graham?" Jackson asked.

"He has a question about dimensions," I replied.

They started talking and I shut my eyes and put my earbuds in. I started getting into this esoteric rapper named TruthSeekah. Every line was about Christian Mysticism, or Magic, or Sacred Geometry, I'd never heard of a rapper talk about this sort of mysticism, let alone rap about it. He could sing too. Just then, I felt a nudge on my arm. I opened my eyes. It was Jackson.

"Hey brother, do you mind if we switch seats so that I can keep talking to this guy, it's kind of hard from where I am," he said.

"Ugh, alright," I said.

We switched seats and this put me right next to Larisa and Jean who were deep in conversation. I put the earbuds back in and continued to relax until I heard through the earbuds that we were beginning to land. I kept my eyes closed and my ear buds in, completely ready to have my ears pop and pain in them like I usually do. Only this time, nothing. I fell into the trance of the music.

I was shaken awake by Larisa.

"Bro, you slept through a landing? Who does that?" She asked.

"Sorry," I said as I yawned. I reached up and brought everybody's bags down, and we started to walk down the runway.

"So Jackson, I see you made a new friend," Jean teased.

"When's the wedding brother?" I asked.

"I can use you both as dumbbells, keep it to yourselves guys. No, but he was a very interesting guy," Jackson said.

Rosette and Larisa laughed.

"Don't be sensitive, Jackson," Larisa said.

We made our way down the runway and walked across JFK to the air train. After 20 minutes we jumped on and after another 20 minutes we jumped off at Jamaica.

"Alright guys, now all these trains going west are going to Penn Station, so it doesn't matter what train we get on, just pick one that doesn't have too many people on it so we can sit together," I said.

"In New York, that's never going to happen," Rosette said.

"Yeah, the trains here are worse than Boston," Jean replied.

"Fine, let's just get on one," I said.

We waited another 15 minutes until a train pulled up with the red neon sign saying "PENN STATION' on it. We got on and we were on our way.

After Another 25 minutes, we were at Penn Station. We walked up the stairs and went into the giant lobby. The one thing about the Big City that I came to find was that it was nowhere near as clean. It wasn't quite Summertime yet, so it wasn't going to smell like liquid garbage, but all the same. After half an hour, we decided to get something to eat. As we were sitting there, a familiar face came up to us.

"Hey guys," Dannick replied.

"Hey brother, how are you?" I asked.

"Doing great. A little nervous about tonight," he said.

"Why is that?" I asked.

"Because what we're doing is very illegal and could get us into a shit load of trouble. Missy took the night shift today, so we have to be there at 7. We've got to get to Battery Park where the Ferry is," Dannick said.

"I thought we weren't taking a ferry?" Rosette asked.

"We're not, but that's where Frantic Missy is going to meet us," he said.

"Who's Frantic Missy?" Larisa asked.

"My ex-girlfriend/fiancé," Dannick advised.

"Why Frantic?" Rosette asked.

"You'll see soon enough. Finish eating, we have to go, it's at the lower tip of Manhattan," Dannick said.

We finished eating and made our way to the subway. I can't tell you how long we were on it, or how many subway lines we changed, but eventually we got to Battery Park. When we got off the subway, we were walking to the steps going up. There was a beer pong table along the wall, and a man was lying on it, butt ass naked. There was another guy set up with tattoo equipment and was tattooing his ass.

"What the hell is this shit Dannick?" I asked.

"You don't have subway tattoo artists in Boston?" He laughed.

We made our way down the corridor and there was a homeless man that grabbed a bucket next to him, pulled his pants down and took a dump into it.

"I think I'm going to be sick," Rosette said.

"You don't have homeless poop sessions in Boston?" Dannick laughed.

"Get me the hell out of here before I kill you Dannick," Jackson interjected.

"Relax, we're almost there," he said.

"Another thing Jackson. When early steam ship locomotives came out, they believed that women's bodies weren't designed to go at 50 miles an hour; they worried about the many dangers of traveling at such high speeds and one of their concerns was that a train ride could cause a woman's uterus to fly out of her body," I said.

"Interesting. I'm assuming you forgot to take your ADD medication this morning," Jackson replied.

We walked up a few flights of stairs and there we were. It was roughly six in the evening, the sun had gone down and we were at the dock. We just had to wait for Missy to come pick us up. To think, we thought we had all the time in the world.

What has been will be again, what has been done will be done again; there is nothing new under the sun.
—Ecclesiastes 1:9

What profit has not that fable of Christ brought us.
—Pope Leo X

Chapter Eleven

"Did you know that the IMF World Bank and ten countries held a simulation of global financial systems collapse led by Israel, sensitive data was 'leaked' to the dark web and went viral," I said.

"Does everything really go back to the financials?" Rosette asked.

"If you'll notice, and I'm pretty sure I've said this before a few times, they always crash the stock market in Libra," I said. "Also, it's why all saviors in all history are always hung between two thieves. The punishment for stealing. However, on a deeper level, the two thieves are regret from the past and fear of the future. Krishna Mithra hezus of the druids has an elephant on one shoulder and a lamb on the other. Odin has two ravens, one represents thought, one represents memory and though he loves one the most, it's the other he fears will never return," I finished.

"I never knew any of that," Jackson said.

"Missy just texted me, she'll be here in 10 minutes," Dannick said.

"Great," Jean replied.

"Hey Graham, did you know there's a number called Graham's number which is a number so big that if you try and grasp that number, the entropy of your brain will exceed the maximum possible limit it can hold, and your head would collapse into a black hole?" Jackson asked.

"Typically, I stop counting after 69," I replied as I fuddled with the mini TV that I had brought.

"Why did you bring a TV, Graham?" Larisa asked.

"Just wanted to see if anything interesting happened while we were in New York," I said as I turned the TV on to Blur's channel.

Louis Le Prince filmed some of the earliest motion pictures using a camera that he had built. However, he mysteriously vanished. Edison later took credit for inventing the first moving-picture camera. Le Prince's son Adolphe, who believed his father was murdered, appeared in court against Edison. Two years later he was found dead.

"Well, we all knew Edison was one of the biggest assholes to ever live," I said as I turned off the pocket TV and put it in my vest.

"What about the people who have never listened to Blur. Or who think he's crazy?" Rosette asked.

"Only close-minded people get offended because their belief set is so rigid when questioned they feel pain and discomfort from the effects of cognitive dissonance," I replied.

"Five minutes y'all," Dannick said.

I nodded back.

"Gold is the money of kings; silver is the money of gentlemen; barter is the money of peasants; debt is the money of slaves. Norm Franz said that and it's so true. We are all slaves to this. I don't know what this is all leading to, but we definitely need to figure it out sooner than later. I'd hate to be shot again," I said.

"Ludwig von Mises said that many who are self-taught far excel the doctors, masters, and bachelors of the most renowned universities. I think that's what makes this so unique, Graham. You never took to religion, but you were exposed to it. You're not 'damaged goods' or have a Master's in theology. This is why your work is so unique. And how we've been able to tie this all together to some great plan in the world that the elites are playing by is quite amazing," Larisa said.

"It's definitely God's language. If protons were 0.2% more massive, they would be unstable and decay into neutrons. That would end life because there would be no atoms. If the protons grew, it would depend on if the electrons respond and get bigger to counteract it. They're the ying yang of all atoms. It's just a perfect science that we even exist," Jackson said.

"Actually, protons don't really decay either, it's theoretical that they decay at all," Dannick said.

"That's right!" Jackson replied.

"Wait, back to the elites. What do you think they're all doing in Agartha right now?" I asked.

"Ruling us up here from there," Jean said.

"Right? God, there has to be something that we can do," I replied.

"I have been impressed with the urgency of doing. Knowing is not enough; we must apply. Being willing is not enough; we must do. DaVinci," Rosette said.

"We are doing. Right now, we're waiting for a boat," I replied.

Just as I was saying that, a small boat pulled up on us.

"Hey guys, come on board quick, I can't have people seeing you on here," Missy said.

"It's nice to finally meet you," I replied.

"Likewise. Get down in the cabin until I say you can come out. Come on, all of you!" she said.

We all got down in the cabin. I pulled the mini TV out of my pocket again as we took off.

"What are you doing Graham?" Jackson asked.

"I don't boat well," I said

Remember when the Panama Papers came out and revealed that all the rich people in the world are part of an enormous criminal conspiracy to dodge taxes and hoard stolen wealth in offshore accounts and literally nothing happened except a reporter working on the story was assassinated? Yeah, those were good times.

I turned the TV off.

"You get sick in the water?" Jackson asked.

"Sometimes. I have no idea why I turned that TV on to be exact.

"What do you think we'll find when we get there?" Rosette asked.

"Well let's think about this. We can't all go to the Statue of Liberty. Jackson and I will get off and search the torches, and then come back with whatever it is," I replied.

"Wasn't it Henry Ford that said, 'It is well enough that people do not understand our banking and monetary system, for if they did, I believe there would be a revolution before tomorrow morning?" Jackson asked.

I nodded my head. I was starting to get nauseous. I put my head in my hands.

"Here take this Newsdon," Rosette said.

I looked up.

She had a Dramamine.

"Isn't this going to make me sleepy?" I asked.

"It shouldn't. I use it all the time for my vertigo when I get water in my ears from swimming," she replied.

I popped the pill in my mouth and dry swallowed it. She was right. Within 10 minutes I was feeling better.

"Alright guys, you can come up now!" Missy screamed.

We walked up the stairs and onto the boat.

"Man, you guys are so lucky that's it's still dark early enough here. Another few hours and I wouldn't have been able to take you," Missy said

"How long have you been with the Coast Guard?" I asked.

"Oh, a few years now. Makes me feel like a badass," she replied.

"Yeah, you're such a badass," Dannick replied.

"Honey, I'll kick you right over the ledge of the boat, don't start with me. OH SHIT! Graham, can you handle the wheel for a minute," she said as she ran off to the cabin.

"See why they call her Frantic?" Dannick asked me. "By the way Graham, you know that your speech from the TD Bank Arena went viral on Aquastream right?"

"What do you mean?" I asked.

"Some people recorded it and posted it. Some say it's being translated to other languages," he replied.

I hadn't thought back to that night due to the situation that happened later on that night. But it was nice to know information was getting out there.

"You know Dannick, Voltaire says that every man is a creature of the age in which he lives, and few are able to raise themselves above the ideas of the time. To be honest that's how I feel sometimes when I talk to Jews, Christians and Muslims. I feel like I'm in Ancient Greece trying to explain to them that Zeus is an allegory, a metaphor, and that he's not real," I said.

"Haha, Voltaire is also the person on his deathbed when asked by a priest to renounce Satan said 'now, now, my good man, this is no time for making enemies.' Yeah, see that's the part I don't get. If these people are comfortable and confident in their beliefs, then your work shouldn't rise any anger or disparaging remarks. If it triggers them, maybe they should do some soul searching on the house of cards that they rest their faith in. As Thomas Sowell says, people will forgive you for being wrong, but they will never forgive you for being right, especially if events prove you right while proving them wrong," Dannick replied.

"We are starting to see some things getting better. For instance, Daniel's Hosting was hacked by King Null from Anonymous. He uploaded a copy of Daniel's hosting stolen database on a file hosting portal. This is throwing the dark web into a frenzie," Larisa added.

"I have no idea what any of that means," Dannick replied.

"There's nothing more dangerous than someone who wants to make the world a better place. I believe that was Banksy that said that," I replied.

"See I believe that, and I believe that we're collectively ascending our consciousness. But then I remember things like Brazil and France almost going to war in 1961 because they had a disagreement about Lobsters," Jackson said.

"Wait, what?" I asked.

"It's called the 'Lobster War.' Both nations mobilized their navies as they argued over whether lobsters crawl or swim to determine fishing rights," Jackson finished.

"Well yeah, an individual can be bright, but the more people that join the group, the lower the collective consciousness goes. It's why you speak to crowds in catchy slogans that rhyme. Groups of people are panicky monkeys," Rosette advised.

"So true girl. Ugh, where the hell is Missy?" Dannick asked as he went down into the cabin.

We laughed.

After about 30 seconds, he came back up.

"Guys, she's gone," Dannick said.

"What do you mean gone?" I asked.

"She's gone. I don't know where she went?" Dannick said as he combed over the entire boat. He made his way to the back of the boat where he yelped.

"Gross, pervert," we heard a voice say.

I ran over to him and looked down and laughed. Missy had tied herself to the boat and was sitting pants down hovering over the water.

"What? You want some too?" She asked.

"What are you doing? You scared the shit out of us. Why are you dangling off the boat?" Dannick asked.

"Isn't it obvious dick?" She asked.

"We have a cabin. You could have used the bathroom inside," I said.

"Ew, God no, there was a spider in there," she said.

I laughed.

"I'll see you shortly, come on Dannick," I said.

"No, I have to make sure she doesn't fall off," he replied.

"You don't have to stay here perv," she replied.

"Suit yourself king, I'm heading back," I said.

After a few minutes, she emerged from the back of the boat and untied the rope that was tethering her to the boat.

"So here's the deal, I'm going to pull up very close to shore. You're going to jump down, and I'll keep circling. If you don't see me, just wait, I'll be here eventually," Missy said.

"Thanks a lot Missy. Larisa, hand me one of those walkie talkies," I said.

Larisa pulled two mini walkie talkies out of her purse. "Whatever you do, do NOT mention statue or Liberty. People will be able to tune in to this frequency, these aren't very good, but they are long range," she said.

Jackson took one of them and put it in his coat pocket. We jumped down and made our way. I turned around to see the boat taking off. The time was ticking, we just didn't know it yet.

Paper money eventually returns to its intrinsic value, zero. —Voltaire

Chapter Twelve

March 18th
9:45pm

"Come on Jackson, get that lock off," I said to him.

"I'm working on it brother," he replied.

Jackson grabbed a log off the ground, cocked back and came full circle directly into the lock. It opened and flew off. I'd hate to be on the receiving end of that.

"Alright, we're in brother. "Rosette, we're in," he said into the walkie talkie.

"Hear you loud and clear," she replied.

We made our way inside. I hadn't been here since a school field trip in middle school, so I was a little rusty with the layout. We walked around for a few minutes until we came upon it. A giant torch.

"Alright Jackson, turn your phone flashlight on, and see if we can find something here. Search the entire room," I said.

"Roger that," he replied.

We searched the entire room for the next 20 minutes, but we didn't find anything.

"Shit, this isn't good. You know what that means?" I asked.

"That we have to go up?" he asked.

"Exactly," I replied.

Just then we heard a noise behind us. Just as quick as we heard it, it disappeared.

"It's probably a rat or something, let it go," Jackson said.

"Alright so where to?" I asked.

We searched the area until we saw a set of stairs. We started to walk up, until I saw something etched onto the railing.

Weaving Spiders Come Not Here

"Hey Jackson, come take a look at this," I said as I shined a flashlight on it.

"What does that mean?" he asked.

"Remember the Big Heaven Room?" I asked.

He nodded.

"It's their motto," I replied. "We've got to hurry,"

"STOP WHERE YOU ARE RIGHT NOW!" A voice shouted behind us.

We spun around and came face to face with a rather large man aiming a gun at us.

"WHO ARE YOU, AND WHAT ARE YOU DOING HERE?" He demanded.

"OK, calm down, we can explain," I started.

The man shot the gun in our general direction. My heart jumped from my throat to my ass. This was not a security guard here. I'd also had my fill of being shot.

"Come down from where you are," he said as he positioned himself behind us. He began to lead us to the front.

"Sit," he said as he pointed to two chairs.

We complied.

Just then he came up to us and took out some zip ties. He tied our hands to the chairs.

"Who are you and what do you want?" he asked as he cocked his gun back and aimed it at Jackson.

"We're here to pick up something that we left on our trip here earlier," he replied.

"Bullshit," he said as he put his flashlight on and aimed it at us. "Hey I recognize you. You're Graham Newsdon aren't you?" He asked.

I sat there with a blank stare on my face.

"That's fine, you don't have to answer. Once I kill you both and dump you in the water, I'll come back to retrieve what should have never been set here," he replied.

"And what is that exactly?" I asked.

"Shut up," he replied as he turned around and dialed a number on his phone. He started to walk away from us.

"Yeah, believe it or not, Graham Newsdon was here when I got here. Yes sir, I understand completely. I will get rid of the two of them, get what we've come for and the trail will be dead forever. No, thank you sir for the opportunity. I won't let you down," he said as he hung up the phone and walked over to the railing where we saw that phrase. He took out a pocketknife and carved over it so nobody could recognize it. He placed the knife back in his pocket and smiled. He turned and pulled a pack of cigarettes out of his pocket, shuffled it and took one out. He started walking back towards us and lit the cigarette. As the light from the lighter illuminated the room, his eyes grew wide as Jackson leapt towards him with his belt in his hand and wrapped it around his neck. The cigarette fell onto his shirt and the cherry exploded into a million little pieces. Though he was large, Jackson had the leverage, and as he choked him, the man slowly stopped flailing, until finally he just lay there, limp. Jackson then went into his pockets and took out some zip ties and zip tied his hands behind his back. He then took his belt and tied it around a pole to his neck. When this man woke up, he wouldn't be able to move, or barely breathe.

"Jackson, get me out of these," I screamed.

"Oh right, sorry brother," he replied.

"Dude, how did you get out of them?" I asked.

Jackson smiled. "It's a military trick for this situation. I rotated my hand and shifted my body so that I
could take my belt off. Then I tied the belt to my foot
and the other side to the zip tie. Stomp your foot and the
zip tie explodes off," he replied.

"I've got to try that sometime. What are we doing
with this guy?" I asked.

"Leave him there; they'll find him and arrest him in
two days when this opens back up," he replied.

We made our way up the stairs. When we got to the
neck of the statue, there was a hatch that leads to a narrow passage for the torch into the right hand of the
statue, up to the wrist.

"Brother, I'm too big to go up, you have to do this
on your own," Jackson said.

"Alright then," I replied.

I lifted the hatch and went into the torch. It was incredibly windy up there. I made the mistake of looking
down for our boat, which I saw. It would be by the entrance in about ten minutes, and judging by the trip it
would take another 30 to come back. I got dizzy being
up there and sat down for a second. When I sat down,
that's when I saw it. It was a small box with a lock on
it. I looked around for a key but couldn't find one. I
picked it up. As soon as I picked it up, it started to thun-
der and lightning. I ducked back down the small

corridor and the hatch, closing it behind me. I made my way down, met up with Jackson and we ran to the front where we waited a few minutes for Missy to pull the boat around. We climbed up onto the boat. Just then it started pouring.

"Get into the cabin guys, I'll get us out of here," Missy said as she hit the gas. We ran down into the cabin. Completely soaked.

"I'm gunna get sick now, great," Larisa said.

"You'll be fine," I said as I picked up a raincoat from the bed and handed it to her.

"What is it?" Jean asked.

"I don't know yet. Do we have a hammer to get this off?" I asked.

Jackson went to the corner where there was a toolbox. "No hammer, but I have an idea," he said as he took out two wrenches and walked towards us. "Give me the box," he said.

I handed it over to him.

We watched as Jackson worked the two wrenches into the lock. Then applied opposite forces on them and the lock popped right off.

"Remind me never to mess with you," Jean said.

"Thanks brother, but it's simply manipulating forces. Turn one left, turn one up and it causes tension," he said.

"Well, open it," Rosette said.

I opened the box and there was a scroll in it. I unrolled it.

The secret you seek is in a land where people don't speak. A crafty endeavor could mine the secret treasure. Forbidden knowledge abides where a fist and a pen thrive. Though they try and shut it down, it will be the downfall of their crown. The Scales of Libra stand tall, the book will guide you to justice for all.

"We need to go somewhere where we can figure this out. Can you tell Missy to get us back on land, I can't think on a boat," I said to Dannick.

He nodded and pulled his hood over his head and went up to talk to her.

Just then I noticed it at the bottom of the scroll.

It was the constellation Scorpio and a constellation next to it.

"Hey guys, what do you make of this?" I asked as I showed them the engraving.

"What do you mean?" Larisa asked.

"Yeah, that's Scorpio. So what? It's the betrayer. Are we going to get betrayed?" Rosette added.

"What are you thinking brother?" Jackson asked.

I had no idea what it meant, or why I kept seeing it, but it seems to be that I'm the only one who's recognizing it. The constellation next to Scorpio was the Butterfly Nebula. It was right there, in plain sight, etched on to the scroll.

"We've got to get to a library," I said.

"We're 20 minutes out," Dannick said as he came downstairs soaked.

"Libraries are going to be closed," Jackson said.

"Fine, a hotel room at least," I replied.

Jean got on the phone and called the closest hotel to us and made a reservation for three rooms. It was about midnight now. We had two days to crack this, and we didn't even know it yet.

There exists a shadowy government with its own Air Force, its own Navy, its own fundraising mechanism, and the ability to pursue its own ideas of the national interest, free from all checks and balances and free from the law itself. —Senator Daniel K. Inouye

Chapter Thirteen

"Yes, I understand. Yes, he is an eternal pest isn't he. Well, we're not going to make the same mistakes as those before us. If they're not there in two days, they will never find it. Take out their lifeline. Yes, that's exactly what I mean," the man in the black suit said as he slammed down the phone.

Fortunately, some are born with spiritual immune systems that sooner or later give rejection to the illusory worldview grafted upon them from birth through social conditioning. They begin sensing something is amiss and start looking for answers. Inner knowledge and anomalous outer experiences show them a side of reality others are oblivious to, and so begins their journey of awakening. Each step of the journey is made by following the heart instead of following the crowd and by choosing knowledge over the veils of ignorance.

—Henri Bergson

Chapter Fourteen

March 19th
1:45am

> **The secret you seek is in a land where people don't speak. A crafty endeavor could mine the secret treasure. Forbidden knowledge abides where a fist and a pen thrive. Though they try and shut it down, it will be the downfall of their crown. The Scales of Libra stand tall; the book will guide you to justice for all.**

"So, a land where people don't speak. It could be talking about the Shaolin Monks?" Larisa asked.

"What about the mining part. I mean geez, that could be anywhere," I replied.

"The downfall of their crown? Could they be talking about a Church in England? The crown is in England and a Church is silent," Jean said.

"Yeah, but the Scales of Libra stand tall; this has to be somewhere that has a giant statue of the scales. Larisa, can you look it up real quick?" I asked.

"On it," she replied.

"Wait, what about where the fist and a pen thrive?" Jackson asked.

We were silent.

"Anybody have an idea?" Rosette asked.

Again, we were silent.

"What about you Dannick, what do you think?" I asked.

It was silent.

"Dannick? Where the hell is Dannick?" Larisa asked.

Just then Missy came in the room from the adjoining room in a towel, drying her hair.

"Do you feel better now that you've showered?" I asked.

Before she could answer, Dannick came in behind her.

"Idiot, I told you to wait 10 minutes before you come in here," Missy said.

"I'm sorry," Dannick replied.

We sat there staring at these two. Dannicks spikey hair was now flat on his head.

"Did you two take a shower while we're here trying to figure things out? Together?" Rosette asked.

Dannick lowered his head.

"What about all that talk about how Missy was Frantic Missy and that she was crazy and yadda yadda," Larisa said, still pounding away on her computer.

"You're still calling me Frantic Missy you loser?" Missy said to Dannick.

"It's not what you think," he replied.

"Look, I don't care what you two do on your free time, but do you think you can help us figure this out?" I asked.

They both looked down at the ground.

"I'm sorry," Dannick said.

"Me too," Missy replied.

"Dannick what do you think of this?" I asked.

The secret you seek is in a land where people don't speak. A crafty endeavor could

mine the secret treasure. Forbidden knowledge abides where a fist and a pen thrive. Though they try and shut it down, it will be the downfall of their crown. The Scales of Libra stand tall; the book will guide you to justice for all.

"I'm sorry Graham, but I have no idea," Dannick said.

"What about you Missy?" I asked.

"Huh? She said as she was drying her hair.

"Can you take a look at this and let us know what you think?" I asked.

"Ok, ok, sorry. Hair's wet, don't want to catch a cold," Missy said.

"Looks like you caught a dick instead," Rosette said.

Missy grilled her. Then she smiled. She then made her way to the scroll and read it a few times. Then she sat down on the chair and closed her eyes.

"Well, what do you think? I asked.

"I need a minute to think," she replied.

We kept talking trying to figure this out until Missy pulled out her phone.

"We need to get to Merrick in Long Island. I have a friend there that can help us out," she said.

"What do you mean Merrick?" Jackson asked.

"Where a fist and a pen thrive. I've seen that once in my life. My good friend Ash is a Minecraft lunatic. Right at the beginning of the 'Forbidden Knowledge Library' there is an image of a giant fist holding a pen. Thing is, I don't know how to get there without her," Missy said.

"Well, what's so special about this?" I asked.

"It's a forbidden library of knowledge. The governments can't take it down because of how it was created. There's all sorts of information in there that wouldn't come out in the mainstream media, or even alternative media. It's all hidden in books there. I'm sure this is what we're looking for," Missy said.

"A crafty endeavor could mine the secret treasure. It's not a mine. It's a crafty mine. Or Minecraft," Jackson said.

We all looked at Missy.

"Finally, I'll text Ash, but we won't be able to go there tonight, it's too late and they have two kids. We'll have to go first thing in the morning, so I suggest we get some sleep," Missy said.

"Great, I'm exhausted anyways," Larisa said.

"Any luck Larisa?" I asked.

She shook her head. "No Scales of Justice in any Churches in England," she replied.

"Alright, I'm going to bed. And no, Dannick, you're not coming with me," she finished as she turned around and walked into the other room.

"Did she just use me?" Dannick asked.

Jackson walked past him and put his hand on his shoulder. "Happens to the best of us kid," he said.

We all settled into our rooms and set the alarm for early. Tomorrow was going to be a busy day. We had no idea the kind of information we were going to find in this forbidden library. To be honest, I'm surprised I hadn't heard Blur talking about it.

People who say it cannot be done should not interrupt those who are doing it. —George Bernard Shaw

Chapter Fifteen

March 19th
7:45am

"Alright, everyone get in the van. We got the OK from Ash to go there now, they both have off today so it works out well.

We piled into the car and made our way towards the Long Island Expressway and then the Southern State Parkway. After about an hour and a half, we were finally at Ash's house.

"Wait here a sec, let me go get her," Missy said.

She got out of the car and went up to the door. She rang and knocked on the doorbell. Who does that honestly? After a moment or two, Ash came to the door and gave Missy a big hug. Her giant dog jumped on her as well.

"Alright guys, come in, we're good," Missy said.

We got out of the car and made our way to the front of the house. One by one, Ash greeted us with a warm smile. A petite brunette. Makes you wonder how someone that tiny squeezed out two kids.

We made our way to her den where she had a gaming chair and computer system. She didn't mess around.

"Alright guys, what do you have for me?" Ash asked.

"Forbidden knowledge abides where a fist and a pen thrive," Rosette said.

"Ah riddles, love them. Yes, I've seen them before. It's in a secret in Minecraft. There is a section called the uncensored or forbidden library," she said.

"What do you mean forbidden?" I asked.

"It's a 'reporters without borders' kind of thing," Ash replied.

"So, it's illegal?" Larisa asked.

"It's not illegal, it's just beyond the scope of the power of the government. It's a giant library that took 24 builders from 16 countries to build it. The first book when you walk in welcomes you to the library of reporters without borders. Here, let me show you," Ash said as she went to work.

We sat there for a few minutes as she loaded it up. As her avatar started to walk towards it, we saw it.

"There's the fist with the pen," I said.

"In a land where people don't speak. That's brilliant. Nobody talks in Minecraft. It wasn't talking about a physical place, it was talking about the online world," Jackson said.

"A crafty endeavor could mine the secret treasure. It was talking about Minecraft," Jean said.

"We know Jean," Rosette said as she rolled her eyes.

Just then Ash's husband came into the room. He was completely tatted up, wearing a Blink 182 shirt and had an apron over it.

"I made you guys some muffins!" he said.

"Joey, what, this isn't the time," Ash said.

"I'm sorry, I just figured your friends would be hungry after being up all night and getting up early today," Joey said.

"I'll take a muffin," Jean said.

"Here you go," Joey said beaming with pride. "So, what are you guys doing?" he asked.

"No offense Joey, but again, now's not the time," Ash said.

"Aw, can't I help boohbah?" Joey asked.

"No," Ash replied.

"Alright, well, just give me a little kiss and I'll get back to the kids," Joey said as he approached Ash.

She rolled her eyes and gave him a kiss.

"One more," he said.

"Joey, I'm telling you, that if you don't get out of here, I'm going to staple your nuts to your stomach and then run DOOM off of it," Ash said.

Jackson choked on his muffin laughing.

"I'll see you guys later, it was really nice to meet you," Joey said as he turned the corner.

"Are you guys always this friendly to each other?" I asked.

"As long as I've known them," Missy replied.

"I'll press an F for that girl," Ash replied.

"Huh? I asked.

"Nothing, it's a gaming, nothing, nevermind. Anyway, we're here. What do you want to do?" Ash asked as she started to give us a tour of the entire library.

I'd never seen anything like this built before. This was truly a marvel, room by room we went through the entire library. It took over an hour. As we were beginning to get overwhelmed with the number of books we would have to read there, we saw it.

"The Scales of Libra stand tall, the book will guide you to justice for all," Rosette squealed.

"Go the book in this room," I said as I looked around the Egypt room that we were in.

"Makes sense that it's in Egypt, right? I mean, that's where the majority of the Bible comes from, right?" Jackson asked.

"Well, yes and know. The Epic of Gilgamesh is where the flood story comes from, Abraham and Sarah come from Brahma and Serasweti in Hindu. It's really an amalgamation. But as far as current day religions, you are correct," I replied.

"What does the book say?" Larisa asked.

"The press freedom situation is becoming more and more alarming in Egypt, with frequent waves of raids and arrests. Egypt is now one of the world's biggest jailers of journalists, with some spending years in detention without being charged or tried, and others being sentenced to long jail terms or even life imprisonment in iniquitous mass trials. Ever since Gen Abdel Fattah el Sisi seized power in a coup in 2013, a process of "Sisification" has been under way in the media. The government has waged a witch-hunt against journalists suspected of supporting the Muslim Brotherhood and has brought up the biggest media groups to the point that it now controls the entire media landscape and has imposed a complete clampdown on free speech. The Internet is the only place left where independently reported information can circulate, but more than 500 websites have been blocked since the summer, including many news sites and more and more people are being arrested because of their social media posts. Many media outlets have been forced to close because they could not survive economically after being deprived of online visibility. A draconian legislative arsenal poses an additional threat to media freedom. Under a terrorism law adopted in

August, journalists are obliged on national security grounds to report only the official version of 'terrorist' attacks. New cyber-crime and media laws enshrined government control over the media demand made it possible to prosecute and imprison journalists and close websites for sharing independently reported information online. Journalists and human rights defenders are meanwhile banned from much of the Sinai region and from providing independent coverage of any military operation. Coverage of many economic subjects, including inflation and corruption, can also result in imprisonment. The presidential election and the referendum on a longer presidential term intensified the censorship and accelerated the pace with which media outlets are closed. Foreign media are also targeted, with articles being blocked online or attacked by officials, and reporters being expelled or banned from visiting Egypt," Ash finished as she took a sip of water.

"Jesus Christ, and there are books like this for every country in here?" Larisa asked.

"Yup. The truth is that the government in the United States is absolutely furious because they can't shut this down. It's decentralized. Like I mentioned, 24 people from 16 countries created this. So they bury it and never talk about it, but if you want to get your information out there, here's where you come to do it, or hide it," Ash said as she took another sip of water.

"Though they will try and shut it down, it will be the downfall of their crown. It's a metaphor, very biblical I have to add. I got it. But we still need to find what we were looking for here. Are there any other books in here?" I asked.

"No, unfortunately not," Ash said.

"Well, it has to be here. Can you circle the room and see if you find anything hidden or out of place?" I asked.

"Like a secret door?" Ash asked.

"Exactly," I said.

"HONEY! The baby knocked over the tray of muffins and the dog is getting into them!" Joey shouted from the other room.

Ash rolled her eyes. "I'm going to castrate him. Seriously, you're going to see me on the news," she finished.

"I'll go help, you stay here," Missy said as she took off.

We watched as Ash navigated the entire room. Little by little, she checked the walls, but there was nothing. After an hour of doing this, she stood up.

"I'm running to the bathroom real quick. Let me know if you guys have any other ideas," she said as she left.

We sat there and talked amongst ourselves. We had no great idea, and, for some reason, we felt that time was running out. I sat in her chair and guided the character over to the giant Scales of Libra within the Egyptian room. There was a little door with a latch on it.

"When you're done cleaning that up, please make them lunch," Ash shouted at Joey as she made her way back to us.

"You got it boohbah," he replied.

Ash rolled her eyes.

"It's ok, we've all been there girl," Rosette laughed.

"Ain't that the truth," Larisa said.

"Ash, we found something. Is there a way you can unlock that?" I asked.

"I can try one of my keys, but I don't know if it'll work," she said as she tried. After a minute or two it didn't work.

"Can you check in the scales if there is a key in there?" I asked.

Ash climbed it, and, low and behold, there was a skeleton key in the scales. That's why it had been lop-sided. When we removed the key, it went back to being even. Ash went back down and unlocked it. There was another book.

Where the water is black, you will find Sophia. A turbo penis enters her holy vagina once a year. Where the two points meet.

$$\mathcal{X} \ \daleth \ \mho \qquad \omega \ \daleth \ \varepsilon \ \daleth$$

"Great," Jackson said.

"We can figure this out, it's not so bad," Rosette said.

"Where the water is black, where is the water black guys?" Jean asked.

"In your toilet?" Rosette laughed.

"Rose, come on," I said. I have to admit, that was pretty funny though.

"Sophia the goddess?" Jackson asked.

"Sophia is the Goddess of wisdom. The Divine Feminine from Black Goddess to World-Soul," I finished.

"Could that be the black water? Her tears?" Larisa asked.

"She actually represents the feminine aspect of God," Rosette said.

"So, her holy vagina then, sex once a year? No thank you," Larisa replied.

Jean smiled.

"We get it Jean, good for you. Any thoughts?" I asked.

"What if the water is a body of water. The Red Sea is red due to the Sun . . ." he began.

"And the Black Sea is Black due to the night," I said. "Good job Jean,"

"Hey guys, if it's the black sea, that's right near Bulgaria," Larisa said as she fiddled on her computer.

"What about it?" I asked.

"Sofia is the capital of Bulgaria. It's right near the black sea. It's a play on words," Larisa said.

"What about the penis entering the vagina?" I asked.

"A turbo is an anagram for Utroba," Ash said.

We looked at her.

She minimized Minecraft and pulled up a browser I'd never seen before.

"Sorry guys, I can't show you this on Google or even Duck Duck Go. They are both compromised. OK, so as you see here, Utroba is a very vaginal looking cave in Bulgaria," Ash finished.

"Does it say anything about a penis?" I asked.

"Hold on hold on, I'm reading. No, it doesn't. Oh wait, it says here that one day a year, the Sun comes into the cave in a phallic shape and hits off the wall in the back somewhere. I think that's what you have to do is find out where it goes," Ash said.

"Great, so what day does it do that?" I asked.

"Hold on, hold on, ok it says here on the Spring Equinox," Ash said.

"Oh God," Jean said.

"Why, is that a bad thing?" Ash asked.

"Aside from it being my and Hannah's birthday it's in a day and a half. Jean, get the plane ready," I shouted.

"Right away," Jean said as he took out his phone and made a call. Just as he dialed, my phone started ringing. It was Hannah. It was going to have to wait, we had little to no time at all here.

After a minute or two, Jean came back and looked confused.

"What's going on Jean?" I asked.

"Mon ami, I called the pilot who always picks up for me, but it went directly to voicemail twice," Jean said.

"Let's just hope he's in the bathroom or something," I replied.

Just then my phone rang again. It was Hannah. I put her on speakerphone.

"Hi everyone, Graham, pick up when I call you," she said.

"Someone's in trouble," Jean said.

"Shut up Jean," Rosette said.

"Are you watching Blur right now?" She asked.

"No, we just cracked the code with help from Missy's friend Ash," I said.

"Who's Missy? Who's Ash?" Hannah asked.

"We know them through Dannick. We'll explain later, we have to fly into Sofia," I said.

"You're not flying into anywhere Graham," she said.

"What do you mean?" I asked.

"Turn on the TV," she replied.

We turned on Blur

The best we can tell from the intel that we have right now is that two planes were blown up at Logan Airport just a short time ago. One was a Aqualine airbus, and the other was a plane registered to Jacques Solex. As it stands, nobody was killed in the Aqualine airbus, but one person died in Jacques plane. We're getting reports that it's not his son Jean Solex, but rather the pilot of the plane. We'll report more details as it comes to us. Thanks for watching.

Jean dropped his phone and sat down on the chair and put his head in his hands.

"I'm so sorry Jean," Larisa said as she hugged him.

"That pilot was like a second father to me," he replied.

"You know they blew up the plane in order to make it seem like it wasn't just targeted at us," I said.

"What are we going to do now?" Rosette asked.

"We have to keep going. We have a day and a half. Larisa, can you get us tickets to Sofia?" I asked.

"I don't know if there will be any direct flights," she replied as she started on her computer again.

"We're flying out of JFK. They have direct flights literally everywhere," I said.

She nodded.

While Larisa worked on getting us tickets, we realized that there were people that knew we were on to them and were trying to keep everything secret. After all, if we missed the Spring Equinox at the cave, we'd have to wait another year. I had a very bad feeling about this; but as usual, even after being shot multiple times, my curiosity got the best of me.

With prices skyrocketing, the finger-pointing has arrived. While there's plenty peripheral blame that's certainly warranted, problems are not solved by tinkering at the periphery. You solve problems by going directly to the source. The source of inflation is always the Fed. The Fed was granted by Congress the unconstitutional power to counterfeit dollars out of thin air. Until this immoral practice is revoked and once again forbidden, the problems of inflation will never be solved.

—Ron Paul

Chapter Sixteen

The man in the dark suit put his winter coat on as it's always freezing where he is. He always wondered why they couldn't run things from the Caribbean. However, this was how it's been done for generations before him and will be done for generations after him. He sunk into his chair and answered the phone.

"Yes?" he asked.

"There has been a development. They seem to be headed to Bulgaria. Their plane was blown up as per requested, but they are flying commercial," the voice said on the other line.

The man sat back in his chair and rubbed his beard.

"They'll never make it by noon, but all the same, I want you to personally go there and make sure nothing is disturbed," he said.

"Understood," the voice on the other line said.

"Oh, and one more thing," the man said.

"Yes?"

"Bring a gun. Take one of the clean ones," the man said.

"Thank you, sir," the voice said as they hung up the phone.

The man sat back. These bastard kids had already done so much that he wondered if he should just order to have them killed. No, that would be a disaster as their leader was already a household name with quite a move-ment behind him If they were going to kill him, it was going to be in the cave. There would have to be a major event though. Like a collapse of the cave. This got the man's juices going in his head as he began to think about ways to rig the cave to explode. Just then, he picked up the phone and dialed out.

"White House, how may I direct your call?" A young lady's voice on the other end answered.

"I need to speak to the top," the man said.

"Sir, I apologize, but the President is busy right now," she replied.

"I don't care if he's busy, tell whoever you have to that I have to speak to Celtic immediately," the man said.

"One moment please," the woman said.

Celtic was the President's code name. Only those in the in would have known about it.

"This is Bedpine, who am I speaking to?" The President asked.

"It's me, Josh," the man said.

"Oh. I wasn't expecting to hear from you until the Big Heaven Room meeting later in the Summer," the President replied.

"I'm aware. Listen, there's a situation in Bulgaria. I've already dispatched someone to handle it. The other thing is that the President is still technically alive, and if he wakes up, you'll be gone. We need to accelerate the timetables," the man said.

"Understood. How much?" The President asked.

"4.5 trillion," the man said.

"I don't know if I could get public support for that," the President said.

"You're not going to be getting any support at all ever again if you don't figure it out," the man said.

"Alright, let me see if I could put my team on it and find a way to spin this," the President said.

"Tie it into the war in Ukraine. The Russians will love that," the man said.

"That's a possibility. We need to worry about optics though," the President said.

"Rope Vanguard and Blackstone into it. Get the media heads on board," the man said.

"What about Yemen, Somalia and Syria?" the President asked.

"Nobody gives a shit about them. Not your best play, the man replied.

"We'll need a catalyst," the President said.

"Play the humanitarian angle. People have been looking for something new to pin on their social media," the man advised.

"That just might work. It'll be a few weeks before we can put a bill forward. We have to gin up agitation," the President said.

"Damn it, we might not have a few weeks. Everything is collapsing. We need to get it back under control," the man said

"If I may sir, what are you so afraid of?" The President asked.

"It's this Newsdon kid. He's made a game out of ruining everything. I'm so sick of this little fuck," the man said.

"Sir, why can't we just take him out?" The President asked.

"Too public a figure. Back in the day with Lennon, MLK, JFK, Hendrix, it was easier. Now there are camera phones everywhere and he has a world-wide fanbase. No, it would have to be an accident, and I'm not seeing anything right now for it," the man said.

"Well sir, as H.G. Wells said, 'Countless people will hate the New World Order and will die protesting against it.' " The President said.

"Thank you Celtic, I know that quote full well. Don't forget who you're speaking to right now," the man said.

"Mea culpa signore," the President said.

"Don't pull that Italian shit on me either," the man said angrily.

"Sir, what are we going to do with Dotplum?" The President asked.

"He's in a coma. He's locked up pretty tight. There's nothing we can do that wouldn't raise suspicion," the man said.

"Alright, sir, I'll get to working on this right away," the President said.

"Oh, and one more thing," the man said.

"What's that?" The President asked.

"Your payment is due," the man said.

"Don't worry, sir. A Lannister always pays his debts," the President laughed.

"Be well Celtic," the man said as he hung up the phone.

The man sat back in his chair and looked out the window. Snowing again. He slammed his fist down on the desk. Just then he picked himself up, walked out the building and down the street to another building where he walked in and shook the snow off his hat. He walked down the hall and opened the large double doors. There was one man sitting inside armed with an AR 15.

"Thought those were going to get banned in America soon?" The man laughed.

"Good to see you, sir. Your usual stroll?" the man with the gun asked.

The man in the hat nodded.

"Be well," he said as he sat back down.

The man opened a door and walked in to a 20,000 foot warehouse filled to the brim with servers. A cooling system kept the room at a cool 65 degrees. The costs were astronomical to maintain this room, but what did he care. He owned the money of the world. At least, he hoped nothing would change that. That Newsdon kid though.

Great things are not accomplished by those who yield to trends, fads and popular opinion.

—Jack Kerouac

Chapter Seventeen

March 21ˢᵗ

4 a.m.

I woke up to Rosette in my face. It scared the shit out of me.

"Hey old man. Happy birthday," she said as she gave me a hug.

"Yeah, happy birthday Graham," Larisa said.

"Happy birthday brother," Jackson added.

"May all your dreams and wishes come true Graham," Dannick said.

"Thank you for party rocking," Jean said.

We all looked at Jean.

"Je suis desole, but everyone already took all the good ones," Jean said.

"It's ok," I said as I let out an enormous yawn, "What time is it?"

"It's about 4 in the morning. We'll be landing within the hour," Rosette said.

"Great," I said as I stood up and stretched.

"Guys, we're about to land; please sit up and put on your seatbelts," one of the stewardesses said to us.

"Roger that," Jackson said.

Over the next half an hour we slowly started to descend. I put a piece of gum in my mouth, but it only moderately softened the popping of my ears. I feel like I'm in a constant low-grade S&M relationship with flying.

We landed after another 30 minutes and got off the plane first. Jean had a car waiting for us, which we got in. We put the GPS on. It was just more than 3.5 hours away. The womb cave that is.

Everyone started talking to one another about this, but I fell back asleep. I needed my rest.

I woke up to us stuck in traffic at road construction. Great. I looked at my phone, it was nearly 8 am. We HAD to be there as it turned noon to see where it led, or it would be lost for another year.

"Can we take any backroads?" I asked.

"Not if you want to get there in one piece. These aren't the kinds of places you want to wander from," Jean said as he continued to inch up.

Two hours later, and we were still 45 miles out.

There was literally nothing we could do; we were just going to have to tough it out.

March 21st
11:25 a.m.

We pulled up as close to the cave as we could get. We walked the rest of the way there. They're not kidding. From the outside this cave looks exactly like a vagina. There's even a rock where the clit should be. I snapped a picture of it. The sun was nearly overhead now.

We made our way into the cave, and there was a policeman with a gun by the entrance. He tipped his hat to us. Once inside the place was tremendous. Mostly rock, but there were some beautiful carvings into the rocks. I recognized the esoteric and religious iconography of the carvings. There were some that I didn't. Seemed like a foreign language to me made up of symbols.

"Hey Dannick, you're into symbols, right? What does that say?" I asked as I pointed to a section of the wall.

"That's Enochian, Graham," Dannick said.

"Enochian?" I asked.

"As in the language of Enoch," Dannick said.

I had decoded the Book of Enoch with astrotheology in one of my online presentations, but it never occurred to me to search deeper. I looked over to my left, and there was a woman leading a small group of people.

"The Utroba Cave. It's a Thracian sanctuary carved around the 9th or 10th century BC. It was done to

114

represent the vagina of the Goddess. It's 22 meters deep, and there is an altar here as you can see that represents the cervix or the uterus of the goddess. Every day at noon, light enters the cave from an opening in the ceiling, projecting the image of a penis onto the ground. However, today is a very special day. Only this day of the year, the spring equinox, the penis extends all the way to the altar, symbolically fertilizing the goddess's uterus before the spring sowing," the woman said.

"Excuse me miss, hi. Where does it reach to exactly? Where does it meet?" I asked.

"Oh, give it ten minutes and you'll find out," the woman smiled as she turned away.

We waited the ten minutes, and sure as shit, the light came in and met.

"Look, look right there, guys," I said as I pointed to it.

Everyone huddled around.

"Where the water is black, you will find Sophia. A turbo penis enters her holy vagina once a year. Where the two points meet.

115

"What does that say Dannick?" I asked.

"What makes you think I know?" Dannick replied.

"I recognize the symbols. Look, they're all over the wall!" I expelled.

"Ok, hold on a second, my Enochian is a little rusty," Dannick replied.

After ten minutes the guard started getting nosy and came up to us.

"Is there something I can help you kids out with?" He asked.

"No, we're fine. I don't suppose you know what this means?" I asked.

The man shook his head and walked back to his post. Right before I turned around, out of the corner of my eye, I saw him release the latch of his gun.

"Guys, we've got to hurry," I said.

"Why is that?" Jackson asked.

"I think that guy knows we're up to something," I replied.

I turned around and looked at the man and smiled at him. He waved back, smiling which immediately disappeared.

"Come on Dannick, what's it say?" Rosette asked.

"Calm down guys, it isn't that simple, some of these symbols can mean two letters, I need a little more time," Dannick said.

The man kept watching the woman with the tour group. My guess was that he was going to approach us once they left, and they started making their way to the exit.

"Dammit!" Larisa said.

"OK, OK, it says," as Dannick was messing with his phone.

"What?" Jean asked.

He stopped and looked at us. "DIG HERE," he said.

"Fine by me," Jackson said as he looked around for a stick or something. He walked near the back of the room and found a large rock. He picked it up and brought it back to where we were.

"Ready?" Jackson asked.

"Ready!" I replied.

Jackson cocked back and hurdled the rock into where the points meet. It shattered and exploded.

"Hey! What are you guys doing?" The man asked.

"Nothing," I replied.

"I'm going to need you to leave now!" He shouted back as he made his way towards us.

"Dig guys!" I said as Jackson and I turned to face the man.

Slowly the cop reached for his gun. It was at that exact moment that Jackson picked up a rock, cocked back and launched it at the cop. It hit him square in the chest, causing him to drop his gun, which fired a round. Everybody ducked down and the people on the tour ran out screaming. The cop hit the floor and Jackson sprinted towards him as he was standing up and speared him to the ground. He grabbed the baton from his belt and choked him out until he was sleeping. Then, he lay him down on the ground and rolled him over, took out a pair of handcuffs from his belt and cuffed him. He then grabbed the man and sat him up against a large rock.

"This guy is going to have such a headache when he wakes up," Jackson said as he turned around.

"I think I need some help," the tour guide said as she was clutching her arm.

My eyes raised in horror. I ran over to her. I took her hand and removed it from her arm.

"You're very lucky, this just grazed you; you should be fine," I said as I helped her up. Then I had an idea. "Maybe you can help us with something here. Are there any mythologies or stories about this cave that you know of?" I asked her as we walked to join everyone.

"No, not that I know of," she replied.

"What about the carvings on the wall?" I asked.

She was silent.

"If you know something, it could really help us out," I said.

"Supposedly there is a panel behind one of them; when accessed I do not know what happens," she replied.

"Alright guys, what did you find?" I asked as I looked down. My eyes got wide.

"It's a chest. From the looks of it, it's incredibly old," Rosette said.

"Well open it," I replied.

Jackson reached down and brought the chest up to the surface. Jackson worked on opening it. It would be literally the last thing we expected to see.

Whether or not we believe in survival of consciousness after death, reincarnation, and karma, it has very serious implications for our behavior. —Stanislov Grof

Chapter Eighteen

"You know that certain linguistic anthropologists think religion is a language virus that rewrites pathways in the brain and dulls critical thinking?" I asked.

"Did you know that a whales vagina is large enough to walk through?" Jean asked.

"I don't even want to know why you know that," Larisa said.

"I don't understand why this always happens to us. Why we're always hunted down. I've been shot at, attacked by crazy people. For what?" Jean asked.

"Have you actually been shot yet?" I asked.

Jean looked at me and put his head down.

"That's what I thought. All of this has to be leading towards something. You always follow the money. Big business is what wins in the end. Cancer is too big to fail, yet they'll never publish any of Dr. Sebi's work. Or the fact that Vitamin B-17, spending time in an orgone chamber, apricot seeds, avoiding alkaline foods and sleeping in an oxygen chamber works, or THC. I mean Christ, Don Phillips, who was a Design Engineer at Lockheed, part of the CIA and USAF talked about how there are remote control sized devices that can cure cancer immediately," I replied.

"I've read up on some of that. You really have to dig in the dark web to find this stuff," Larisa said.

"Well, there's a website called Bibliotecapleyades where it's all listed. It's the best website to go down any rabbit hole you want," I replied.

"There's no cure for cancer," Jean said.

"Of course there is. The Orgone machine was invented in the early 1900's. Why do you think no US President has died of cancer since Ulysses S Grant in 1885?" I asked.

"It's always about the money and the control, isn't it? Who decided that we have to pay rent to live on a planet where nothing else does?" Rosette asked.

"You want a rabbit to pay a mortgage?" Jean asked.

"No dumbass. I mean, who decided that we were all going to have to buy into this 'money' system?" She asked.

"I think that the top of the top elite illuminati families, the ones that control everything are torn right now between a single world order, or a polarized global power structure that allows for a continuous war situation like we've had. My brother once told me that at the time that the US has been at war 228 years of the 246 years," I replied.

"War is good for business," the woman replied.

"Damn right it is," I said.

"Got something guys," Jackson said as he opened the chest.

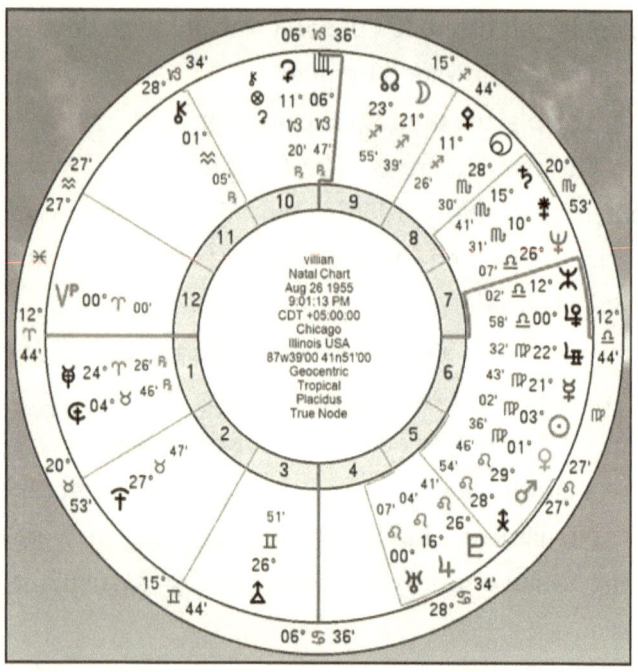

"What's that?" Rosette asked.

"It's a birth chart it seems. Why would a birth chart be in here and who's is it?" I asked.

The woman shook her head, "I can't believe what I'm bloody seeing right now."

"What else is in there?" I asked.

Jackson reached down into it and pulled out some cut out numbers. He handed them to me, and I laid them down.

8 8 9 8 1 6 1 3 3 0

"What's this now?" Larisa asked.

"I have no idea," I replied

Jackson reached down and pulled out a very archaic key. He looked at it and handed it to me. He then looked down into the box and lifted it up and shook it. There was nothing left in it. He threw it to the side.

"What do you think the birth chart is about?" Rosette asked.

"I don't know, but we have to have it analyzed. I'll call Priscilla in a few. What about the numbers?" I asked.

"Anyone have a clue?" Larisa asked.

"They have to be in some kind of order for us to figure it out I'm thinking," Jackson said.

"Very well. Larisa, can you mess with your phone and see if you can find a pattern in this," I replied.

Just then the man in the handcuffs started stirring. The woman we were with noticed it and made her way over to him. She slapped him across the face.

"So you're here to kill us? Is that right?" She asked.

The man stayed silent.

"No matter, you're not going anywhere. Who do you work for?" She asked.

Again, the man stayed silent.

She looked over to us and shook her head, then turned back to the man.

"Well, we'll see what you have in your pockets," she said as she tried to reach into his left pocket. The man violently shook, leaving her unable to get into it and tried to stand up.

"I don't think so friend," the woman said as she knocked him back down to the ground. "Get up one more time and I'll make you sorry you've come here. Did you know that they were coming here today? Is that why you brought your gun?" She asked.

Again, he was silent, but had an angry grimace on his face that could have peeled her skin back.

"I know I've seen these numbers before, I just don't recognize how," I said.

The woman looked back at the man, then made her way to us.

"Put them in numerical order, let's try that," she said.

0113368889

"Still nothing," Rosette said.

"I'm out of answers here Graham, I'm not seeing anything," Larisa said.

I walked over to the man on the ground.

"You know something, don't you?" I asked.

The man looked at me silently.

"Whether you like it or not, we're going to figure out who sent you," I said as I smiled at the man.

He looked back at me and smiled with blood in his teeth. He turned and spit the blood onto the ground a foot away from me. I turned back disgusted and walked back to my friends. I looked at the numbers and looked at all the carvings on the cave to see if anything made sense. I started playing around with the numbers until I saw a familiar pattern.

"Hey guys, check this out!" I shouted as I rearranged the numbers.

1.618033988

"I'll be damned," Jackson said.

"What? What is it?" Rosette asked.

"It's the first ten numbers of Phi," Jackson replied.

I turned back to look at the man in the handcuffs. His eyes were wide now, and he was breathing heavily.

"What is Phi?" Jean asked.

"Phi is one of the two numbers in our universe that never end. They're not from our dimension," Dannick replied.

"What do you mean?" Larisa asked.

"They never end. Graham, look at that!" Dannick said as he pointed to the wall.

I turned and looked. There was a square with the Phi symbol on it. I walked over to it and analyzed it. Looking over the entire wall with all the symbols, I pressed the block that the Phi symbol was on. To my surprise it sunk into the wall, and we felt some rattling. Just then another cube on the other side popped out. I walked over to it and noticed that it was hollow. I looked inside it and found a scroll in a bottle on a latch. I took out the bottle and the latch snapped shut. Just then another cube came out of the wall and had a clock that was counting down from 15 minutes. Just then, 11 chests came out of the wall, each numbered from one to eleven. Shit, what have I done.

"Jackson, come help me with this thing," I replied.

Jackson came by, took the bottle which was very thick and slammed it on the ground. The bottle cracked and the scroll fell out. He picked it up and showed it to me.

The key that you hold is a skeleton key and will open each one of these boxes. However, only one of them will stop the countdown to the destruction of the cave. It will also hold the key to where you will go next. Only with the great understanding of Phi, will you be able to figure out which box to open. If you guess incorrectly, the cave will immediately collapse, keeping this secret buried forever.

I looked over at the countdown. We have 13.52 left.

"Guys come on. Box 1-11. Which one?" I asked as I dangled the key in my hand. I looked over to the man in the handcuffs and his eyes were huge. He kept trying to stand up, but the walls and floor was shaking, and he couldn't. Some light debris started to fall from the ceiling.

"1.618033988. Closest whole number is two. Maybe that's it? Box two." Larisa said.

"It can't be that simple," I replied.

11:43 left

"Come on guys, anything?" I pleaded.

Nobody had any answers.

"Maybe we should just get out of here," Dannick said.

"Dammit no! You heard what it said, it'd be lost forever!" I cried.

"Graham, the first ten numbers in Phi add up to 47, maybe it's four or seven? Rosette said.

"But if you add the four and the seven again you get 11. Add them together you get two!" I said, as I thought we figured it out.

7:34 left

I walked over to the man on the floor. I dangled the key in front of him. "You will die here with us if we get this wrong, I suggest you help us!" I shouted.

The man turned his head to the side deflated and turned back to us. "I have no idea what you're talking about," he said.

"Ugh," I said frustratingly as I made my way back to everyone.

"So, its closest number is two and they all add up to two. I'm going with two," I said.

I made my way over to the second box and I was about to put my key into it when Dannick shouted scaring me to death.

"Don't do it!" he shouted.

"Why not?" I asked.

"You're right we needed to add up the numbers, but you're wrong about the number," Dannick said.

"We all know how to add Dannick," I said as debris continued to slowly fall around us.

"No, you don't understand. This is numerology," he replied.

"What is?" The woman asked.

"Yes, the numbers add to 47 which reduce to 11. But that's where you got it wrong," he said.

4:13 left

"Now would be a good time to explain Dannick," Jean advised.

"In numerology numbers reduce to 0-9. However, if you get an 11, you don't reduce that. It's known as a master number. 11, 22, 33. These are all master numbers. Yes, the clues lead you to box two, but it's not. It's box 11," Dannick finished.

"You're sure about this? Rosette asked.

Dannick looked at her.

"Because we're all dead if you're wrong," Larisa replied.

"You don't reduce 11. It's box 11," Dannick replied.

I shook my head and walked over to box 11. A giant stone fell from the ceiling and almost crushed me. I put some pep in my step.

"Guys, you all might want to get out of here while I do this," I advised.

"We're here with you brother, just do it," Jackson said.

I looked over at everyone and they nodded. I was so lucky to have such a loyal group of friends.

"Here we go," I said.

I put the key in the lock of box 11 and turned it. The walls started to shake violently for a moment and the lump in my throat shot down to my ass. Just as quick as it started to shake, it stopped.

"Dannick, remind me to buy you a beer when we get home," I said.

He smiled.

I looked over at the man on the floor who seemed relieved. Also, it seems like he urinated on himself. Charming.

I opened the box and pulled it out of the wall. Suddenly, the other boxes disappeared back into the wall. I looked inside.

Just as the Phallus into the vagina on the 'day of the pass over' at high noon, so shall the cave reveal another secret in the midnight Devil's Eyes.

"Great. Does anybody have any idea what this means?" I asked.

The woman we were with shook her head.

Just then we heard a chirp coming from the back wall. We turned to see the man had somehow loosened his belt and pulled the walkie talkie off it and was screaming into it.

"Guys, we've got to get out of here immediately," I said, as I watched the man maneuver his hands to the gun and aim it at us.

"Grab the scroll Jax, RUN EVERYBODY!" I said as we took off. The man waddled towards us firing shots in our general direction. We all got into the car and took off down the road.

"How the hell did that happen?" Jean asked, as he drove down the road.

"Just keep driving. We have to ditch this car and get a new one," I replied.

"On it," Larisa said as she started working on her laptop to rent us a new car.

"Don't use my card baby; they blew up my plane they're probably tracking where Graham and I spend money. Put it on yours," Jean said.

Larisa nodded.

Just then we heard the faint sounds of sirens. They were too far away from us to catch up, but if this guy that was sent to kill us was half good at his job, he would have noticed our car.

"There's a dealership half an hour away," the woman said.

I turned around to see her in the back. I completely forgot about her.

"I'm sorry I had to bring you into this," I said to her. "I'm Graham Newsdon," I said to her.

"Bellatrix Rigel, pleasure," she said.

We had to figure out what that scroll meant and what the deal with the birth chart was. Also, unfortunately for us, we weren't going to be able to leave Bulgaria yet, while we had people looking after us.

Prior to the creation of Christianity, women were considered mans equal. Pagans still believe this is true.
— The Crone's Grove

Chapter Nineteen

Walter Reed Hospital, ICU

President Josh Bedpine made his was down the corridor with the secret service following suit. He made his way to the front desk of the nurse's station.

"Good afternoon," he began.

A nurse looked up at him and dropped her pen when she saw him.

"Mr. President, it's nice to see you. What can I do for you?" She asked.

"I'm here to see the President," he replied.

"I'll take you right over," she said.

She got up and left the nurse's station. She took them down a windy corridor where there were some guards outside of a room at the end of the hall. She smiled at them.

"At ease gentlemen," the President said.

"Mr. President," one of the guards nodded.

The two men separated and allowed for him to enter. The secret service lined up behind him.

"Not here boys, I think I can handle this on my own," the President said.

The secret service nodded to one another and stepped back. The President opened the door, walked in and closed it behind him.

President Bedpine looked around the room. There were many stuffed animals and balloons, with dozens of cards written on the shelf. He turned his focus to the President, who was intubated, eyes closed and breathing rhythmically. President Bedpine sighed to himself and then quietly pulled up a chair to the President. He ran his thumb over his eyebrow and turned his focus on the President.

"You had to push buttons with the Central Banks didn't you Dotplum," he began, "I heard about it right away. Believe me, there was nothing I could do. I'm assuming you got the men in black come pay you a visit when you first got elected like I did when I took over for you. They sat you down and explained to you what you can and can't do? This is how it's been done for over a hundred years, they say. Then, oh boy, when you tried to buy that country, you crossed a red line with them. The only reason you're even moderately alive is because when they poisoned your diet coke, they didn't expect the diet coke to have been expired. You only took a sip. Could you imagine if you finished the whole thing? Look, I don't want to play politics with you; we have worked together for a very long time, and I was honored when you selected me as your VP, but you can't cross these men," the President said as he looked over at the former President.

"I don't know why I came here to tell you this or why I expect you to wake up. I've set in motion for another 'loan' from these people in order to finance the latest war. I suppose this will be my legacy. Pundits are saying that my popularity is literally tied into your popularity. If the American people ever woke up to how things were truly run, there would be hangings in the street. I'll have you know I had to reverse your proposed tax on the Federal Reserve and your offer to buy that country. The truth is, I would love to sit behind the scenes while you get things done, but I ended up getting a call from the man that runs the world, can you believe that? He called the White House directly and used my code name. Definitely a power move. He let me know he wasn't messing around. I've got a family Rand, I can't afford to be taken out. I just hope that wherever you are, whenever we meet again, you can forgive me," the President said as he put the chair back. He looked at his friend and former President, clasped his hand and took out a piece of paper from his pocket that his daughter made for him. He opened it up. It was a white butterfly sitting on a flower. He placed it in his hand, stood up and made his way out of the room.

Just as the door closed on the inside, the former President pinky started to twitch. The current President had made a grave Kinsley gaffe.

Truth is coming, and it cannot be stopped.
—Edward Snowden

You shall know the truth and the truth shall make you mad. —Aldous Huxley

Chapter Twenty

"Yes, give me some news, good news hopefully," the man in the dark suit said as he cut the tip off a cigar and lit it carefully. "Oh, I see. There was an incident at the cave. With a gun nonetheless. Well, how did that turn out? I see. Wait, so you mean to tell me that you had an opportunity to take them all out and instead they escaped?" the man said as he crushed his cigar and threw it in the garbage out of rage. "This is fine. They have no plane and if they don't get to the second location by midnight it will be lost. Do make sure that happens please?" he asked. "I understand. Keep me posted on your progress. No, if they make it to the second location we will take further action. These bastard children cannot discover what we know!" the man said as he hung up the phone.

The man in the black suit sat back in his luxury chair and looked at his desk. He had a pile of what the media had dubbed as 'super gold' on his desk. These kids had figured a way to disrupt the world's gold market. It was his and his people's responsibility to disrupt the markets. He sat back and poured himself a glass of Louis XIII. He took a sip and sat back and reflected. Things were not going exactly as planned. The former President of America was still alive somehow even though a very Russian tactic was used on him to poison him. The new President was on board with everything, unlike the former, so that was good. A proxy war had begun in Russia and Ukraine. No doubt with both their economies shattered, naturally they would finance both sides of the war. The people in America were so stupid with the media that they controlled. They are just so easy to manipulate and mold their thoughts. Sure, there were conspiracy theorists and those that didn't follow the mainstream narrative, but they would always be seen as outsiders. That was until Graham Newsdon came along and mixed truth with fiction in his book series that took off. The Vatican had been up his ass about taking the kid down, but even they knew that their time was basically up. After all, it is written in the stars. Age of Aquarius. The man in the suit was busy making sure that Jerusalem and Israel were safe in order to enact their next plan, opening a one world religion building in the heart of Jerusalem. He had thought that it would have caused a war when the former President moved the embassy to Jerusalem. He hated the former President. He wasn't supposed to be elected. It was only when he tried to buy the country that he rules it all from that he had to physically step in. That was a close one, but thankfully the media did their duty and silenced the story after a day or two.

The man closed his eyes for a moment and ran a few scenarios in his head. It actually occurred to him that Graham and his team might actually figure out where he is and come to him. If that was the case, he would be ready for them. He had a wide range of people ready to step in at a moment's notice and Dotplum them all. A part of him was intrigued though. What if he got to stand face to face with him? What if it was him that put a bullet in all their brains and then dumped them in a drum filled with acid? He didn't like surprises and this kid had done so much damage already. In a way, he was almost hopeful that he could get to see him face to face. Physically they were no match, but that tall mixed kid would be a problem.

Irrevocable commitment to any religion is not only intellectual suicide; it is positive unfaith because it closes the mind to any new vision of the world. Faith is, above all, openness, an act of trust in the unknown.

—*Alan Watts*

I distrust those people who know so well what God wants them to do, because I notice it always coincides with their own desires. —*Susan B. Anthony*

Chapter Twenty-One

March 21
6 p.m.

"I have to call Priscilla. We need to figure out this chart," I said as I took a look at it once more.

I pulled out my phone and texted her a picture of the chart. After a few moments she messaged me back,

"Graham, I need you to call me about this," Priscilla said.

"Why? What's wrong?" I asked.

"I've never seen a chart like this," she replied.

"What do you mean? What's wrong with it?" I asked.

"It's pure evil. If I could take the worst out of all the charts of other people and put them together into a super villain, it would be this man," she said. Just then she AquaTimed me.

"Hey Pris, so what's going on?" I asked.

"Are you with your friends?" She asked.

"No, hold on a sec, Jean's negotiating a cheap van for us," I said as I motioned everyone to come over.

"OK, so I'll break this down for you as simple as I can," she began, "The big three is Aries rising Sagittarius moon and a Virgo sun. As his three major components of his personality, the elements fire and modality mutable is very dominant. This person lacks air & water. Having only one generational planet in air with a childhood wound Chiron in aqua. Saturn also is in Scorpio in this person's 7th house, and this is where I would like to start this breakdown. Having lack of air and water makes the native have a harder time with logic and reason and balancing out emotional intelligence with reason. Now to the 7th house. The 7th house in astrology is the house of partnerships, business contracts and collaborations of close partnerships, whether marital, family, best friends, or close work partnerships. This placement can be hard in Scorpio. This can bestow wisdom and deep structured connections, but can also limit the native in making connections with what Saturn doesn't want. It is also in Scorpio which brings ties to karmic connections and many transitions and death in close partnerships to the native. For this native having Juno asteroid conjunct tells a story of losing a partner or close friend during Saturn return activation. This can also make the native overbearing, controlling and pessimistic with close contacts, and at 15 degrees it's a Gemini degree showing limitations with close partnerships centering around communicating. This native can be verbally abusive and limit the expression of close partnerships. The native could've experienced many deaths around family members early on that can manifest as adult traumas and the fear of loss or abandonment. We see in the 12th house Pisces is intercepted with Aries having the native's subconscious mind in a state of martyrdom and war. This native feels life is an uphill battle with many raw moments of pain and loss and the sense of drowning in deep waters with the inability to process emotions properly due to the lack of water and air in his chart. The counter house is Virgo with an interception in 6th with Leo and libra influence showing a lot of energy center around health, mental health routines day to day work and conscious processing. There is a lot centered around action's drive ego love learning communicating within 7th house connections and work/career. This person has a powerful ego with Pluto in Leo in the 5th making contact with Jupiter inflates this person's ego for the center stage and power dominance. This native can also be abusive with that Pluto influence being narcissist towards children and or anyone who might have a platform (5th house domain.) With Uranus in Leo in 5th as well the native can be quite eccentric, and ego driven to the point of not recognizing his own vibrational embodiment in accordance with the stage and his platform. Being that this native is an Aries rising, impulses anger and aggression are big themes and something apart of his personality very dominant in the 1st house, which is the lens of how he sees the world and how others see him. He can come off as militant and angry as well as aggressive and a powerhouse being a bold leader and marching forward with decisions impulsively and selfishly as well as a dictator. Jupiter allows this man the expansion of his platform, however Jupiter indicates judgment, and this man uses his platform to pass down judgement on the masses based on darker plutonian influences and creating a philosophy for his regimes. His moon and mercury square meaning his emotions and mind are not in alignment with each other causing a power struggle between processing empathy with logic. Having a sag moon can make him flighty apathetic and self-righteous especially sitting in the 9th house where his philosophical beliefs in life are very much tied into his emotional state and inner guide. The north node is also in the 9th house in Sagittarius, indicating his aim in life is to find his truth in his exploration of foreign countries cultures and world religions. Creating his own philosophical beliefs centered around his influence of his mother as the moon indicates childhood integration of his mother's personality and his experience with her. She could've been fanatical in her beliefs which influenced the native to adopt those emotional biases. His mother's influence isn't the only cause for apathetic emotions, but having Saturn in Scorpio can indicate losing a father or father figure early on in life with repeating themes every time Saturn is activated or having heavy transits. Father could've been very domineering and controlling nitpicky and critical and this influence became this man's inner dialogue. This man's ego is dominated by Virgo energies being all analytical and believing his perfectionism is correct so in his mental conscious mind (6th house rules left brain, logic reason) he serves people to what he believes to be best and doesn't allow to be challenged. He has mercury and Venus in Virgo; Venus being debilitated or in its fall in the sign of Virgo. Making Venus unhappy which corrupts love money and material gains. Venus isn't happy in Virgo as it criticizes, nags and tries to perfect love to its own ideals and apathetic biases. According to FBI data and astrological research, mutable signs have the highest tendencies for psychopathy and serial killer tendencies, Virgo being very high statistically speaking. This native having mars in Leo 29 degree, a critical degree so closely cusp with Virgo for anger and action, Virgo sun for ego and primal urges, and Venus Virgo for very eroded ideals of love and greed with money. Moving on to Chiron in 11th shows childhood trauma and pains around friendships and this native's dreams and aspirations. He had trouble with friends growing up, especially in aqua as a social sign with Chiron indicates a loner and someone who was different eccentric, but wanted to fit in and didn't, so this created a wound with how he connects with the community at large. Not being able to make connections with friends as a child really molded his ideals for his dreams and big goals. The pain created the framework to how he approaches and deals with the collective. Now he has adopted the lower expression of the potentiality of his natal energy. This native has potential for great power and influence, as we all are faced with two paths in life. The native needs deep shadow work to be able to introspect as this person has emotional traumas that limit his ability towards empathy and fairness. 10th in Capricorn indictates a boss and CEO in his field, and a very strict ruler as cap is ruled by Saturn and his natal Saturn shows he rules over his partnerships. Having Lilith conjunct his midheaven shows his reputation as a very provocative leader who can be sneaky tricky while utilizing seduction in his communication. The native can be very seducing with words and gain popularity with people who are the same vibration and/or have a lot of people who don't agree and feel his ruling is tyrannical and dictator. Having Neptune in libra can cause this person to have delusions centered around his connection's contracts and partnerships. His values can be other worldly not being aligned with the times and or very fanatical; he can feel he is some type of mystic to his partnerships and needs to be revered. Might have a god complex with this placement especially making contact to his moon in sag and Jupiter in Leo," she finished.

"Pris, I don't really know what any of that means," I said.

"This man is a psychopath. He has all the tendencies to show for it. I would be extremely careful and tread water with this man. Who is he anyway?" She asked.

"No clue, but we need to figure that out," I said.

"Alright my friends, we have a new car!" Jean shouted.

Bellatrix turned to me "What about that code that we need to figure out? We don't even know where we're driving to," she said.

"You're right. Priscilla, love you, thank you for everything," I replied.

"No problem, let me know if your new friend needs to get her chart read," she replied.

Bellatrix smiled. "I think I'm ok for now. I wouldn't want to find out anything too spooky," she said as she turned to go to the car.

I hung up the phone and we all got into the car. As Bellatrix stepped in, a gun fell out of her sundress and onto the floor. We all looked at her mortified.

"I can explain this guys, I took it off the cop before that was trying to kill you," she said.

"How can we believe you?" Jackson said as he reached his arm out preventing her from getting in the car.

"Because look, this one doesn't have a serial number on it. That man was there to kill you and he didn't want to be caught doing it," she replied.

"He shot at us anyway," Jackson said, firming his arm to keep her out.

"Look guys, I just don't want to be shot at. If it makes you feel better, take it," she said as she turned it around and handed it to Rosette who handed it to Jackson.

Jackson looked over the gun and after a minute, removed his hand. "Fine, but no more surprises," he said as he handed it back to her.

"Jean, I'm a little worried. Your plane blew up, so they must be tracking your cards. All of your cards," Bellatrix said.

"I know. That's why I used cash," he replied.

A wave of relief came over her face.

"Alright so what was that code that you found?" She asked.

Just as the Phallus into the vagina on the 'day of the pass over' at high noon, so shall the cave reveal another secret in the midnight Devil's Eyes.

"Wherever it is, we have to get there by midnight," Jackson said.

"Shit, it's 6:30 right now. Larisa, Rosette, see if you can find something about the Devil's Eyes online," I replied.

"It's a song by Hippie Sabotage," Rosette said.

"What the hell is Hippie Sabotage?" Dannick asked.

"It's a band. That can't be it," Larisa said as she kept looking.

"It's also a song by Penny McLean," Larisa said.

"Guys, it's not a song," Jackson said.

"It's also a movie," Larisa said.

"Can we narrow it down to a place?" I asked.

"It's also a book by Jennifer Loren," Rosette said.

"This isn't helping girls," I replied.

"We're trying Newsdon, we are," Rosette said.

"Why does she call you by your last name?" Bella-trix asked.

"It's just her thing," I replied.

"Here's something. The Devil's Eyes is also known as the Helix Nebula. It looks just like a Red Eye," Larisa said.

"We know everything has to do with astrology, that's the way the underworld and the dark web work," I said.

"It's also when a man looks at a woman in a way telling them they will do naughty things to them," Rosette said.

"Now I'm excited!" Larisa said as she winked to Rosette.

Rosette giggled.

"The Helix Nebula is located in Aquarius," Rosette said.

"Another pointing to the changes that will happen in the Age of Aquarius?" Jackson asked.

"Did you know that numerous magicians and early scientists such as Copernicus, John Dee, and Tycho Brahe were also astrologers for the rich and powerful? When a well-packaged web of lies has been sold gradually to the masses over generations, the truth will seem utterly preposterous, and its speaker a raving lunatic. People have no idea just how deep the changes in Aquarius are going to get, if we don't end this now," I replied.

"It is dangerous to be right in matters on which the established authorities are wrong. That's Voltaire," Dannick said.

"Voltaire again? Why does he keep coming up?" I said.

I had my hand out the window. We hadn't moved yet as we had no clue where to go. It was just then that out of nowhere I felt something land on my hand. My instinct was to shake it, but I looked over and it was a white butterfly. I was in complete shock. This has been following me for a long time now.

"Guys look," I said as I motioned to my hand.

"I've never seen a white one before," Rosette said.

Just then it flew away.

"We're on the right track guys," I said.

"How can you be so sure?" Bellatrix asked.

"I can't explain it, I just know we are. But if we don't figure out where we have to go now, we're screwed. What are the chances it's going to be in Bulgaria as well?" I asked.

"Dammit, we're getting nowhere. I'm going to the bathroom, I'll be right back," I said.

I got out of the van and went into the shady dealership. The man pointed me to the bathroom. When I came out, I had an idea.

"Excuse me hi, do you speak English?" I asked.

"Yes, I do, but not very well," the man replied.

"Understood. We're looking for something called the Devil's Eyes. Do you know what that is?" I asked.

The man turned red. "We do not talk about the Devil's Eyes here. We call it God's Eyes," he said.

"Ok, I'll bite. What are God's Eyes?" I asked.

"It's a how do you say? Tunnel? No. Cave, it's a cave, known as Prohodna Cave. It is almost five hours drive from here. They say that the Moon comes through the eyes and illuminate a secret on a special day," he said.

"What special day?" I asked.

"Nobody knows," he replied.

I looked at my phone. It was 6:45 and we had a nearly five-hour drive. We would just get there in time.

"Thank you!" I said to the man. He nodded back.

I raced to the car and told everyone what I had discussed. Jean put the GPS on his phone as our van was so old it didn't have GPS. He put it in drive and slammed on the gas. We were on the way. It was going to be extremely close, but we should just make it. Little did we know that like Scorpio, we were betrayed already.

Problem is, an individual must have an experience of perturbation at some point in their life that turned their head for good, leaving them with a subtle, sneaking suspicion about the world. Otherwise, this system is set up with safety nets under every accusation we make about it. —Unknown

The vast majority of human beings dislike and even actually dread all notions with which they are not familiar. Hence it comes about that at their first appearance innovators have generally been persecuted, and always derided as fools and madmen. —Aldous Huxley

Chapter Twenty-Two

"He seems to be uncomfortable. I'm going to raise his morphine up slightly," the nurse said to the military guard at the door. Once she finished what she was doing, she left the room. No sooner did she leave the room, that the President started to toss and turn and finally open his eyes.

"Mr. President, can you hear me?" The guard asked.

President Dotplum looked around the room. One minute he was in the Lincoln Room and the very next minute he was in a hospital bed. He sat up a bit to take in his surroundings and yawned. He had a slight taste of almonds in his mouth.

"Where am I?" he asked.

"You're in a secure wing at Walter Reed Hospital," the guard said.

"What happened? I can't remember anything," he said.

"From what we can tell, you've been poisoned. It seemed to have been through your diet coke that you were drinking. Of course, that was left out of the NEWS," the guard said.

"I've got to get out of here," President Dotplum said as he sat up.

"Mr. President, take it easy, you just woke up. You've been out for days," the guard said.

"Son, what's your name?" The President asked.

"Derek," he replied.

"Well Derek, if you want to keep your job, help me up out of this," the President said as he ripped the IV's out of his hand. Blood started to trickle down.

"Mr. President, you're bleeding," Derek said.

"I can see that. Get me a gauze and my clothes. Where are my clothes by the way?" The President asked.

"They should be in the closet, here, let me get them for you," Derek said.

The President turned his body and put his feet on the floor. He had a pounding headache and when he tried to stand, he slipped a little. Derek had to catch him.

"Don't worry son, I'll be fine, just help me get dressed. I have to get to the White House," the President said.

"Why are you in such a rush?" Derek asked.

"That's classified," the President advised.

Derek helped the President get up on his feet and helped him get dressed. He fixed his tie and his hair for him and bandaged up his wrist.

"Are you sure you want to do this Mr. President?" Derek asked.

"Just get the car ready and let the White House know I'm on my way in," the President answered.

"I don't understand. Shouldn't we let the doctors check you out first?" Derek asked.

"I appreciate your concern, but please don't question me again," President Dotplum replied.

Derek chirped into his walkie talkie and asked the people guarding outside the door to clear the hallway. After a few minutes, he heard back that it had been cleared.

"We cleared the hallway, and we're good to go. We can't reach the White House right now, there seems to be some sort of commotion," Derek said.

"What kind of commotion?" The President asked.

"Something about rushing a 4.5 trillion-dollar bill through Congress. There's a proxy war that started while you were out sir," Derek said.

The President looked at Derek hard. "We've got to get to the White House now!" He said as he opened the door.

"I don't understand the rush," Derek said as they walked down the empty corridor, "President Bedpine is handling things right now," he finished.

Rand Dotplum stopped walking and turned to Derek. "Son, I know who poisoned me," he said.

"Who Mr. President?" Derek asked.

"I can't tell you right now, but you will find out soon enough. We just have to get back before that damn bill is passed," the President said.

They walked down a few more hallways and into the underground garage where an armored vehicle was waiting. Derek opened the door for him, and Rand got in. Just as Derek was about to close the door behind him, the President put his hand out to stop the door from closing.

"What are you doing son?" the President asked.

"What do you mean?" Derek asked.

"Get in," Rand said.

"Are you sure?" Derek asked.

"I can't trust anyone right now, and I need you to come along with me," the President said.

Derek smiled and got in the back with him. Another secret service agent shut the door behind them, and they were off back to Washington D.C.

"What kind of person would want to poison you?" Derek asked.

"I've made some decisions recently about the country that have angered a lot of the elites and swamp creatures in Washington D.C. To answer your question, only pure fucking evil would do this and subject our country to what they're about to do. Try and get the speaker of the house on the phone for me, will you son?" The President asked.

Derek nodded and pulled out his phone. He didn't have the speakers number directly on hand, so he would have to six degrees of Kevin Bacon it. The President laid back in his chair and took a deep breath. Truth was he wasn't ready to come out of the hospital yet, and his body was telling him that now; but this was a matter of utmost urgency. He closed his eyes as he thought back to what he thought was a dream when Vice President Bedpine came to speak to him. Unfortunately for him, he remembered everything about it.

History records that the money changers have used every form of abuse, intrigue, deceit and violent means possible to maintain their control over governments by controlling money and its issuance. —James Madison

One thing is clear: The Founding Fathers never intended a nation where citizens would pay nearly half of everything they earn to the government. —Ron Paul

Chapter Twenty-Three

The armored vehicle pulled up at the underground entrance to the White House. There was a frenzy of media outside the gate, all reporting that Rand Dotplum was back. The secret service opened the door, and Rand and Derek got out. Rand fixed his suit and walked in past everyone.

"Welcome back Mr. President."

"Are you sure you're ready to come back?"

"It's good to see you Mr. President."

"We're so happy to have you back sir."

The President stopped and turned to address the staff.

"I feel great, maybe greater than anyone's ever felt before, that great. I look forward to continuing my work, just as soon as I have a talk with the Vice President," he said as he turned back and continued walking.

The secret service clouded around him, but he waved them off.

"I appreciate you being here, but I only need my man Derek here for now. Thank you, but I can take it from here," he said.

They continued to walk through the enormous mansion until finally they approached the Oval Office. Rand fixed his tie and walked in with Derek.

"Mr. President. I'm in shock. I didn't expect to see you back so soon," President Bedpine said.

"Thank you for all your diligent work while I was out, but it's time for you to go now," President Dotplum advised.

"Sir, I can't leave my post until you've at least met with the medical staff here and have been given a clean bill of health. We wouldn't want anything to happen to you, it would confuse the public," President Bedpine advised.

President Dotplum looked annoyed. Then turned to address the secret service and all that were in the room, including the photographer who was doing a shot of the President at work.

"I need everyone but the Vice President to leave the room right now," President Dotplum advised.

"But sir, we're in the middle of a shoot," the photographer said.

President Dotplum looked annoyed. "I said leave," he said.

Everyone left the room except the secret service agents.

"No no, you too gentlemen. Get out, I need to talk to the Vice President alone," he said.

The secret service shrugged their shoulders and left the room. Derek started to make his way out of the room as well.

"No, not you son, you stay," the President said.

"Understood," Derek advised.

Once everybody left the room, the President shut the door and turned to the Vice President.

"I don't understand sir, we were in the middle of," he began as he was cut off by the President.

"What have you done Josh?" The President asked.

"What do you mean?" Josh replied.

"I heard on the way here you're trying to pass a 4.5 trillion-dollar bill, with money going to a proxy war overseas? I've worked very hard to keep the debt and deficit down; I'm gone for a few days, and you blow it out of the water. Who put you up to this?" President Dotplum asked.

"You don't understand sir, nobody put me up to this. This is what we do when other countries are in crisis. We tied an infrastructure bill for roads and buildings as well," President Bedpine advised.

"Dammit Josh! You know damn well that the money never goes to roads, the same way that the lottery money never goes to the school system. What happened to my plan to tax the Federal Reserve? Do you know how odd it is that I disappear and then suddenly that story disappears as well?" President Dotplum asked.

"Sir, we just thought it was in our best interest," he began as he was cut off again.

President Dotplum sighed and looked at the floor. Then back up to the Vice President with radiant eyes that could burn a hole through the occult desk that he was working on.

"The gig is up friend. I gave you a chance to come clean now and you didn't. Now I'm going to tell you what happens from here," the President said.

"What do you mean?" President Bedpine shifted nervously.

"When I was in the hospital, you came to visit me," President Dotplum advised.

"I did. I wanted to pay my respects and make sure you were ok," Bedpine advised.

"I heard everything you said to me Josh," President Dotplum said.

"Excuse me?" Bedpine replied.

"I heard everything Josh. I know who poisoned me, or at least ordered it. I know why they did it too. Luckily, I didn't suffer the same fate as Lincoln and Kennedy. Money is the root of all evil Josh, and you are not strong enough to lead this country, or even serve in my office. So, here's what we're going to do. You're going to resign as VP, you can state family issues or wanting to get out of politics, I don't give a shit. But you're out. As of this exact moment I am the President of the United States, and I am throwing out that trillions dollar pile of dog shit and going back to my plan on the Central Bank. We didn't come this far with this opportunity to do right by Americans without having someone spineless as you sit in the space," President Dotplum advised.

"Sir," Bedpine began, "That's an interesting story, but unfortunately it's all fairy tales. I don't know what you think you heard in the hospital, but I can assure you that wasn't it," he finished.

"You're going to play politics with me right now when I'm giving you an out? First of all, GET OUT OF MY SEAT RIGHT NOW!" President Dotplum ordered.

Bedpine froze in his chair. He had never heard the President raise his voice like that.

"Derek, will you help him out," President Dotplum advised.

Derek started making his way over to Bedpine when he stood up and shuffled away from the desk. President Dotplum went to the back and sat in his chair, readjusted it, and placed his hands firmly on it.

"I've given you ample chance to make amends. You've made your bed, now you will have to lie in it. I'm going to convene a federal investigation into my poisoning and make my report known," President Dotplum advised.

"Ok, ok, I will resign. Mr. President, I deeply apologize. I had nothing to do with the poisoning; I was only made aware of it right before it happened. Grave threats were made to my family in case I were to deviate from the plan. Please forgive me sir," Bedpine advised.

President Dotplum sat for a moment and thought of his next response.

"Vice President Josh Bedpine. You have disgraced yourself, probably more than anyone who has ever disgraced themselves before you. It is by the hair on my nuts that I'm still alive and I intend to make the most of it. You acted like all your predecessors by not putting the American people first. I'm going to call you a press conference right now. Go to the Rose Garden, announce my return and your retirement from Politics. I never want to see your face again," President Dotplum advised.

Josh Bedpine lowered his head and walked out of the room.

The President called a press conference as he intended. He was going to walk out with Bedpine to the Rose Garden and give a presser with him.

"Follow me Derek," The President said as he made his way out of the room and followed behind Bedpine about 15 feet back.

They entered the Rose Garden and immediately were greeted by a bunch of flashing bulbs.

"Mr. President, is it true you're back?"

"Mr. President, there are rumors that you were sick, are you feeling better?"

"Thank you everyone for coming. I'm actually here for the Vice President right now. He has something he needs to say," The President advised.

"My fellow Americans, it is by my great and happy accord that I can advise that the President is back from a health scare. I tried to lead the country in his absence, and I have found that it doesn't suit me. It's a lot easier to be behind the scenes than it is to be in front of everything. I have decided to retire from politics and spend more time with my family. I will not be taking any questions as of now, but it was an honor if only a brief time, to be commander and chief," Vice President Bedpine advised as he turned to go back in the White House. President Dotplum remained.

"Mr. President, what happened while you were gone?"

"Mr. President, have you discussed with the Vice President his plans after leaving?"

"Mr. President, what does that mean for your cabinet right now?"

"My fellow Americans. This may come as a shock to you, but I don't like hiding the truth from you. An attempt on my life was taken and I was poisoned. Some of the changes in our policies were the root cause of it and there are some bad people, very bad people, possibly the worst that ever were are behind this. I'm going to be working on bringing them to justice with the full authority and power vested in me. I can't tell you more than that. I can tell you that the 4.5 trillion-dollar bill as of this moment is dead. My policy on the Federal Reserve stands; as soon as we have things worked out, we will begin implementing it. It's time that we started getting rid of this debt that has been poisoning and controlling us from the beginning of the time our country was formed. Just know that I have your best interest in my being. As George Washington said to James Madison back in 1789, no generation has a right to contract debts greater than can be paid off during the course of its own existence. As Julian Assange said, when all is exposed, 98% of Washington will fall. We are going to make people accountable for taking us down a dark and dangerous path. Congressman Charles A. Lindbergh Sr. in 1913 said that from now on depressions will be scientifically created. And he was right. From this moment forward, the Speaker of the House Nadir Stenos will be my acting Vice President. I know him very well, he's a great man who has done an excellent time as his home state's Governor and now a member of Congress. That's all I have for you right now, thank you for your time," President Dotplum finished.

There was a slew of questions coming from the media, but the President motioned to Derek, and went back in the White House.

"Sir, that was incredible, what are you going to do first?" Derek asked.

"First, I'm going to need a diet coke," he replied.

Derek radioed into the walkie talkie and asked for a diet coke for the President.

"A bottle, I'm not drinking open cups anymore," The President advised.

They went back into the Oval Office and sat down. It was just President Dotplum and Derek.

"What are you going to do now sir?" Derek asked.

"The first thing I'm going to do is email Graham Newsdon," The President advised.

"Who?" Derek asked.

"He's a friend, and hopefully not dead yet," The President said as he opened his laptop and started typing away.

Money is the God of our Time, and Schrodhilt is his prophet. —Heinrich Heine

An attack upon our ability to tell stories is not just censorship—it is a crime against our nature as human beings. —Salman Rushdei

Chapter Twenty-Four

Former Vice President Josh Bedpine made his way home. He opened the front door and walked inside. His wife was still at work and the kids were at school. He picked up his phone and dialed the man in the dark suit.

"Hello, this is Bedpine," he advised.

"Josh. I've just watched the news. I'm incredibly disappointed. How did that happen?" The man asked.

"When I went to visit him, he was in a coma. I said a few things to him. Turns out, he was in a coma, but he heard and remembered everything I said," Josh advised.

"Oh, for your sake I hope you didn't mention us or my name," the man hissed into the phone.

"I did not," Josh replied.

"You're on thin ice friend. So, what now? You retired. Why didn't you stay in the White House. We could have used you some more," the man advised.

"It was President Dotplum's idea for me to retire. He told me that if I didn't step down, he would expose everything," Josh advised.

"I see, and what exactly would he expose?" The man asked.

"I'm pretty sure he knows that it was you guys who poisoned him," Josh said.

There was a long pause on the other line while the man thought. "I'm going to have to get back to you," he said as he hung up the phone.

Josh Bedpine's hand was shaking. These were people who he didn't want to fuck around with. He went into his liquor cabinet and pulled out a bottle of sambuca. He poured himself a glass and dropped one ice cube into the middle of it. He waited a minute, stirring the cube around until it cooled off a bit, then took down the glass. He put the Sambuca away and put the glass in the sink. He then went and sat down on his couch in the living room and turned on the TV. All the news outlets were covering his speech and he felt sick to his stomach. He turned the TV off and lay on the couch. He put a pillow over his head and fell asleep.

He woke up to the phone vibrating in his hand. He had no idea how long he had been out. He wiped the sleep from his eyes and picked up the phone.

"There's still work to be done," the voice came from the other line.

"I don't understand. I'm out of the White House. I can't do anything. I'm out," Josh advised.

"YOU'RE OUT WHEN I TELL YOU YOU'RE OUT!" The man screamed into the phone.

"I'm sorry, but I'm moving back to San Francisco with my family," Josh said.

"I don't care where you live as long as you're reachable and you still have contacts in the House," the man replied.

"Just tell me what you want me to do, and I'll do it, but after this, I'm done," Josh advised.

The man was quiet on the other line for a moment. "You know what, you're right. There isn't anything more that you can do on your end. Enjoy Frisco," the man said as he hung up the phone.

Josh started to feel a little better. He wasn't thinking about what kind of work he would do; he made a lot of money on insider trading while in Congress before being plucked to be Vice President. He wouldn't have to work. He went upstairs and started to pack things up, his wife and kids would be home in the next few hours. Eventually he would build up the courage to tell his wife what happened with everything. He didn't like keeping stories from her, but it was the best way to keep her safe.

Just then, there was a knock on the door. He ignored it for a moment. Then he received a text message.

Groceries are here

His wife must have ordered the groceries delivered. He'd never been home at this time, so he didn't know when she had it.

"I'll be right down!" He screamed from the top of the stairs, as he made his way down the stairs, tying a robe around him.

He put his eye to the peep hole in the door. Just as he did that, the man outside noticed the shadow going over the peep hole, placed a ruger directly up to the peep hole and fired a single shot. He heard the man inside slump and fall on the ground. He left the groceries on the front doorstep and got into his car and sped off.

My own mind is my church. All religious institutions are human inventions, set up to terrify and enslave humankind and monopolize power and profit.

—Thomas Paine

Chapter Twenty-Five

"It had to be done. He was compromised," the man in the dark suit said into the phone. "Yes, I understand. No, we haven't been able to find them, they have gone off the grid, or at least, they have gone off using cash only," he finished.

The man in the dark suit hung up the phone and looked around. It was going to be a rough couple of days he felt. The President of the United States was back in power and had managed to undo everything that the late Vice President had been able to do for them. The man in the dark suit shook his head. How did Rand Dotplum even win the election? He was supposed to be there as a joke. He was supposed to lose to the other candidate in splendid fashion. They were supposed to enter the age of Aquarius with a new world order, a new world religion, and soon to be, a new world government when the money collapsed. People were already moving off the United State dollar as the reserve currency. In the past it was simple. When somebody tried that, a war or crisis was manufactured by the talking heads on the TV, and they went in and took them out. Now countries are getting ballsier. This was no good. This was written in the stars thousands of years ago and it was supposed to be his turn to shine behind the scenes of it all. With the 'new' or 'fresh' gold, that the media had termed it, it had drastically fluctuated the value of the gold, and it was that meddling bastard Graham Newsdon and his friends who were directly responsible for that. The man in the dark suit knew that this was a house of cards, built on paper thin nothing that could blow away with the wind should something disrupt it. Now, those kids have gone off the grid, and in all likelihood were on their way to pay him a visit. That was fine, he thought. Nobody seems to be able to take these kids out. Well, he would delight in the many ways to make them suffer. Apparently blowing up the Solex plane that they were using didn't keep them back. There was going to be an end game for this, and he had sworn to himself that the people who made his job difficult, would pay the ultimate price.

We are governed, our minds are molded, our tastes formed, our ideas suggested, largely by men we have never heard of. —Edward Bernays

Whenever you find yourself on the side of the majority, it is time to pause and reflect. —Mark Twain

Chapter Twenty-Six

March 21
9:53 p.m.
"In the year 1367 BC, well before Moses, Akhenaten established Monotheism under a Sun God in Egypt. Early ancient Jews and Christians believed in many Gods, and there have been archaeological fertility Gods from that time period that show the same. Also, the biblical flood which goes back to the Epic of Gilgamesh, but we won't go there, goes back to 540 BC. The Babylonian Enuma Elish has its flood story written around 1100 BC. There is something called the Atrahasis which has its flood story written in 1700 BC and there's an even older flood story from something called the Eridu Genesis which predates Atrahasis. That's stated to be around 2300-3000 BC. The Atrahasis means "Wise One of Exceedingly Wise." He was the King of Shuruppak

before the time of the flood. Now, Mount Everests sum-mit is slightly less than 9km above sea level. For that to be covered with water, well put it this way. The esti-mated amount of water in the oceans, seas, glaciers, and rivers is slightly less than 1.5 billion cubic km. To have enough water to Cover Everest you'd need an estimated 5 Billion cubic km. Even if it rained this much and it all drained in 40 days, where did the water go? It doesn't matter. There are 2487 noted contradictions in the Bible," I said.

"I never thought of things that way. Is this what you talk about in your lectures and Aqua channel on the in-ternet?" Bellatrix asked.

"Yes, and many more. For instance, did you know that there is a measurable flash of light that occurs inside the woman when the sperm is finally let into the egg? The Buddhists believe that it takes seven weeks for a soul to reincarnate on earth. The Jews count the Omer for 49 days. Guess what happens on the 49th day of ges-tation? The pineal gland becomes visible on a sono-gram. You can argue the right to live vs abortion all you want; it doesn't even really matter and personally I don't give a shit either way. You can also say a brain or a heart is needed for life, whatever. The fact is at that flash of light, life begins at conception. And the ancients knew this. We have forgotten a lot of this over time, and most of it is kept from us," I finished.

"Fascinating, what else are you working on?" Bellatrix asked.

"Jean, how far out are we?" I asked.

"About 45 minutes mona mi," he replied.

"Right, sorry about that. There are 12 essential salts in your body. Depending on your Sun sign in astrology, you are deficient in three of them. They cause health issues. It's not your fault, it's the luck of the draw. The Zodiac wraps around the human body. Dannick, you are a Libra which means your kidneys are strong. Based on your weaknesses it could be detrimental. There's a pill called Bioplasma that doses you with all twelve. You'll find your problems clear up. There is a great book out there called the Zodiac and the salts of salvation that explain this better," I finished.

"I was doing some research about a week ago after my tour of the cave was over. A few years ago, the Chinese discovered some Sanskrit documents in Lhasa, Tibet and sent them to the University of Chandrigarh to be translated. Dr. Ruth Reyna of the University said the documents contain directions for building interstellar spaceships. It seems that nothing is as it seems," Bellatrix finished.

"The hardest part of all of this was not figuring out that the world is ruled by people who use Astrotheology against us; I mean don't get me wrong, that was a hard pill to swallow, but the hard part is actually finding out that nothing we think is real in the world through textbooks, education, media, is ever the true story. They're all backed by agendas," I finished.

"We're 10 minutes out," Jean said.

I nodded my head.

"You know, if my writing career and lecture career doesn't pan out, I'm going into music," I said.

"Oh yeah?" Jackson asked.

"You know the song 'I took a pill in Ibiza?' Well, when you start to push 30 it becomes 'I took an edible in my bathrobe," I said.

Jackson laughed.

We talked for a few more minutes then pulled up at the cave. We had about 20 minutes to spare.

We got out and walked inside. There were some people scattered around. The first thing you do when you get in the cave is look up immediately. You'll see two eye shaped holes in the ceiling. The moon was between them right now but would shift in the next 20 minutes showing us what we need to do. After about twenty minutes, the moon started shifting into the right eye of the cave and illuminated it. There was a small section in the rocks that was illuminated more than others though.

"That's where we have to dig," I said as I turned to Jackson. He took his flannel off and wrapped it around his waist. Then hopped down to where it was pointing and started removing the rocks. After about another twenty minutes he spoke up.

"I think I have something here," he said.

We all got closer.

Jackson then pulled out a chest with a 7-digit combination lock on it.

"Shit guys, any ideas?" Rosette asked.

"Can't we just knock the lock off?" Larisa asked.

"This box is so flimsy that if I did that, it would destroy the box and whatever was in it," Jackson said.

Just then we heard the screeching of tires outside and the rustling of a few people running into the cave. It was the same man from the other cave!

"Hey you, stop right there!" He said as he pulled his gun out and aimed it at Jackson.

We froze.

"Do you have any idea how difficult it has been to track you all?" The man said as he made his way towards us.

"What are you going to do?" Bellatrix asked.

"I'm going to take you all in. You'll never see the light of day again," he said, "but first," he continued as he aimed the gun at Jackson.

Suddenly there was a loud crack of a gun. We all ducked down. When we stood back up a moment later, we saw that the man was on the ground, blood pouring out of his right upper arm. I looked up and Bellatrix was standing there aiming the gun at him.

"You shot a cop?" I asked.

"He's not a cop. He's a hitman," Bellatrix said.

"How can you possibly know that?" I asked.

"You paid for the car in cash, we didn't stop the whole way here. He was tied up when we left. How do you think he found us?" She asked.

"You will be caught eventually," the man said laughing and coughing, keeping pressure on his arm.

"We need to kill him," Bellatrix said.

"What? No, don't kill him. Let's just go to the car and figure out this lock," Dannick said.

After a few moments, we convinced Bellatrix to put the gun away and walked out.

"You guys know that he knows our cars license now, right? I can just go back in and," she began.

"No killing," I said.

"Fine," she said as she handed Jackson the gun and jumped in the car. Jackson then walked over to the other car and shot out the front two tires. He came back to the car, and we started going. Where we were going, we had no idea, but we needed to find a safe spot to think for a minute.

The public as a mass does not think, will not defend what it believes and will not analyze the propaganda which is constantly in circulation against any public man who refuses to play along with the gang.

—Manly P Hall

Chapter Twenty-Seven

The man in the dark suit looked at his phone. He got a long text message telling him how the man had been shot and they had gotten away again. He said they had the chest, but it was still locked, and they had no clue how to open it. The man in the dark suit threw his phone across the room and opened a bottle of Patron and poured himself three fingers. He took it back to the face, squirmed a bit, then coughed. He shook his head then pulled out an ice cube from the ice machine, put it in the glass and poured another three fingers. He stirred it around and then took it back. That was much better. He placed the glass on the desk satisfied. He tried to figure out what the next move was now that the US had pulled out of that giant bill which would have edged them closer to World War III. The Americans forget how close Russia is to Alaska and their backyard. The Russians don't care how many men they lose. Everything was going just fine until the President of Russia kicked out the Central Bank from them. It took them a deep false flag and many months of planning with the media to get the people on board with fighting them. The man in the dark suit thought that it was quite extraordinary that nobody put together that all the 'evil' countries that America sees as such are the last ones in the world without a Central Bank. He knew that Fort Knox was empty of Gold, and there were banks in New York City that were housing Vatican Gold that no longer had it there. He was aware that being the Age of Aquarius was the sign of the man. He was on top of the 13 illuminati families, they all took their orders from him. It was his family that ruled everything since the time that the Roman empire 'fell'. Well, technically it didn't fall, it just migrated, and like the Nazis after World War II that migrated to the US and founded NASA, they had moved to their now secret location to run things from. Unfortunately, Graham Newsdon and his friends were hot on his tail and were on their way to figure things out, he just didn't know how much they knew. The man in the dark suit wondered why there had to be a hidden trail that led to him, as it just puts them in a vulnerable situation. Unfortunately for him, this is how it's been done for nearly 2100 years. In the event of a cataclysm, there had to be a path that leads to him, for other members in the 'dark circle' as he called them, to find him. The two glasses of Patron had kicked in slowly and he was feeling rather relaxed. He answered the text message. The truth was, he didn't even know where the next clue would be, but he did know that if Graham ever made it to him, he would take his time with him. Countless people failed trying to take Graham down. One man not even related to the New Order shot and almost killed him. He never expected him to recover, let alone be back on the trail so soon. He was going to take him down and slowly, enjoying every minute of it. He was going to torture and kill him for all the people in the past who had failed to do so. This cat has run out of lives, he thought to himself as he turned on the TV to Blur Slanders, who had been calling the New Order out for years. The only reason he was allowed to stay was that they turned the media and public opinion against him. Plus, he was a Christian, and not knowing what he knew and even Graham knew about the New Order in the Age of Aquarius, he stayed as a disinformation agent according to some. The Age of Aquarius, the Age of the sign of the man. They say that the Age of Aquarius is an age of enlightenment, while the Age of Pisces was the Age of deception. That people would start to wake up, that it was to be a Golden Age. That would not be allowed to happen. It's the sign of the man, the building of the man.

With microchips, neurolink and a One World Religion. Merging with machines even. Give people the ancient gift that was lost over the millennium, the ability to live forever. There was no way that after all those years, it was going to be him who would be taken down. There was too much at stake. He was so close to bringing everyone to a one world currency as well. It was simple, he would forgive much of the debt to all nations if they adopted the one world currency. Unfortunately, crypto had put a damper into it all. It threw a real monkey wrench into his plans. However, as usual, the governments were mining them at record speed and taking them away. It was to the point though that they may have to make everything digital and give people microchips to buy and use things. That was one of the ideas he had.

It was a bit lonely though, most of the 13 illuminati families made their way to Agartha recently, leaving him to carry the bag for the Schrodhilts. It was a tedious process getting everything in order, but in the back of his mind this fucking kid and his friends stood to ruin it. If they ever made it to him, he would take them all down. In fact, just then he had a wonderful idea. He knew that the rich kid, Jacques Solex's son was after him, so he already blew up his plane, now he would take out his father. That should stop them. Graham's mother and father and brother were already dead, but there were others that could pay the price for it. He got on the phone and made a quick call to a high-ranking officer in France. After a few minutes, he hung up the phone. It was only a matter of time until Jacques Solex was dead. That should convince them to stop coming.

Control oil and you control nations; control food and you control the people. —Henry Kissinger

Chapter Twenty-Eight

We pulled over on a busy street. We were hidden amongst the people.

"Alright, does anyone have any idea what the code is?" I asked.

"Try 1234567," Larisa said.

I tried it, no good.

"Next," I said.

"Try the first 7 of Phi," Jackson said.

1618033

"No good either," I said.

"Can't we just destroy the box?" Rosette asked.

"We don't know what's in it, we need to preserve it for the time being. How long would it take to go through every combination of one through seven on this thing Jackson?" I asked.

"Forever," he replied.

"Well, that's no good," I replied. "Larisa, see if you can find out any sacred patterns on your computer while we're here."

"On it," she replied.

"What about Pi?" Jackson asked.

3141592

"Nothing," I replied.

"Come on friends, we need to get to the bottom of this," Jean said.

"I know brother, do you have any suggestions?" Dannick asked.

Jean shook his head.

"Try 1111111, then 2222222 and so on and so on," Rosette advised.

Just then my phone rang. I put it on speakerphone.

"Hi baby, how are you?" I asked.

"Hi Husker," Rosette yelled into the phone.

"Hi guys, are you watching the news?" Hannah asked.

"No, why?" I replied.

"Turn it on ASAP. Is Jean with you?" She asked.

"Yeah, he's right here," I replied.

"Jean, I'm so very sorry," Hannah said.

"Porquoi? Qu'est qui ce passe?" He asked.

"Oh my God," Larisa said.

"What?" I asked.

"Do you see it?" Hannah asked.

"See what?" I asked back.

"Jean your father was murdered," Larisa said in shock.

We were all in shock.

"This is playing all over the news. Blur is all over this story. First his plane, then him. There are no leads so far, but the police are hopeful," Hannah said.

Jean just sat there in complete shock.

"Jean, are you ok?" I asked.

"I haven't talked to my father in quite a long time. The police in France aren't going to do shit," he replied.

"How do you know that?" I asked.

"Because the only people who could get that close to him were the police," Jean said.

"Are you saying this is from the inside?" Hannah asked.

Jean nodded his head.

"I can't hear him," Hannah said.

"Yes, sorry yes Hannah," Jean said as he slumped back into his chair. Larisa wrapped him up in a big hug and Jean let out a little whimper.

"We have to figure this out, I bet it's all connected. The plane, his dad, the cop that found us twice. I don't understand how people keep finding us," I replied.

"I have no idea, but next time they do, I'm going to shoot them dead," Bellatrix said.

"Who's that?" Hannah asked.

"Oh, it's a friend we've picked up along the way. She's an expert on all things Bulgarian I suppose," I replied.

"Well, be safe guys, bring my man back home in one piece," Hannah replied.

"Copy that kittycat," Larisa said.

I hung up the phone with Hannah and we all looked at Jean. We could tell the attention was making him uncomfortable.

"The best way we can honor his legacy is if we move forward and figure this out," Jean said.

"Right, so anybody have any ideas?" Dannick asked.

"What about the Beginning of Aquarius/End of Pisces," Jackson asked.

"What do you mean?" I questioned.

"What if the combination is a date? 12-21-2012?" Jackson asked.

"That's 8 numbers, there are only 7," I replied.

"Oh," Jackson said as he slumped down.

"Maybe it's a date and time? Bellatrix asked.

"What do you mean?" I replied.

"What time was the case made available?" She asked.

I shook my head.

"3-22-0000," she replied.

"What's 0000?" I asked.

"Midnight on 3-21. That's when it became available for us to see where it was hidden," she replied.

I shrugged my shoulders, "Sure, whatever," I said as I punched the numbers in, the lock opened right up. We all looked at her.

"Don't look at me, I didn't put this there," Bellatrix said.

I carefully opened the chest and pulled out a piece of metal that had letter inscriptions on it.

baaba aabbb aabaa babaa abbab ababb aaaab baaba abbab aaaab baaaa abaaa abbaa aabba babba abbab baabb baaba abbab ababa abaaa aabab aabaa baaba aabbb aabaa aabaa babba aabaa baaba abbab ababa aabaa baaba babba abbab baabb baaab aabaa aabaa aaaaa abbaa aaabb baaba aabbb aabaa baaba aabbb baaaa abbab aaaaa baaba baaba abbab ababa aabaa baaba babba abbab baabb baaab abbba aabaa aaaaa abaab baaba aabbb aabaa baaba baaaa baabb baaba aabbb aabab abbab ababa ababa abbab babaa aaaaa abbbb baabb aaaaa baaaa abaaa baabb baaab baaba abbab baaba aabbb aabaa aaaab abbab baaba baaba abbab ababb aabab abbab baaaa baaba aabbb aabaa aabab abaaa abbaa aaaaa ababa baaaa aabaa baabb aabaa aaaaa ababa

"What in the holy hell is that?" Jackson asked.

"I've never seen something like it before," Larisa said.

"Is it binary, like letter binary?" Rosette asked.

"Interesting," Bellatrix said.

We all looked at her.

"I've seen this type of code before, but I can't place what it is," Dannick said.

"I know what this is," Bellatrix said.

"What is it?" I asked.

"It's known as the Baconian cypher," she replied.

"What?" I asked.

"Sir Francis Bacon. It was created in 1605. It's a method of steganographic message encoding. Supposedly he used this cypher to encode messages revealing that he wrote Shakespeares work, or that he may indeed be Shakespeare. It most definitely ties into binary as we know it today," she finished.

"Well, can you crack it?" I asked.

"You have to give me a pen and a piece of paper," she replied.

"Here," Jean said as he handed her one from the dashboard while wiping away a tear from his eye.

After about 20 minutes, we had our answer.

The womb to bring you to life, the eye to let you see, and the throat to let you speak the truth. Follow Aquarius to the bottom for the final reveal.

"What does any of that mean?" Larisa asked.

"I have no idea," Rosette said.

"Follow Aquarius, so we know there's going to be either a statue of a man, or water," I said.

"But what about the rest?" Bellatrix asked.

We sat there in confusion for what felt like an eternity. Then, all at once, it snapped into focus for me.

"Guys, what was the first place we went to in Bulgaria?" I asked.

"The Vagina Cave," Jackson said.

"The womb," I replied. "What was the second place?"

"The Devil's, the Devil's or God's Eyes!" Larisa squealed.

"The eye," I replied.

"What about the throat?" Dannick asked.

"There is a place called the Devil's Throat. It's about five hours from here," Bellatrix said. "It's in Trigrad; it borders Greece."

"Alright, Jean, put in the coordinates," I said.

"Je suis desole, but I don't feel like I can drive right now friends," he said.

"That's fine, I'll drive," Jackson said as he hopped out of the van and into the front seat.

"What is so special about Bulgaria that it's all in here?" I asked as we pulled off into the night.

When a person can't find a deep sense of meaning, they distract themselves with pleasure. —Viktor Frankl

Chapter Twenty-Nine

We drove through the night and arrived at the Devil's Throat cave just as the Sun started to peak above the horizon. We had been up nearly 24 hours and we were exhausted. We got out and sat around the car for a little bit. We were going to let the Sun come up a little more and light up the cave so we could see where we were going. It reminded me of the story of how Jesus put his fingers on the blind man's eyes and then suddenly he could see, which goes back to a story of the Sun, that we are all blind at night, until the Sun comes up in the morning, touches our eyes and allows us to see. After about half an hour, we made our way inside the cave.

"Alright guys, this place is pretty big, and we don't know anything about it, we should split up. I'll go with Bellatrix and Dannick, the rest of you split up," I said.

"Agreed," Jackson said.

We split up and searched the entire cavern. We didn't have much luck until we came upon a large rock and Dannick rested for a minute.

"Promise me that after this, we can get some sleep," he said.

"Absolutely with you on that one brother," I replied.

"Wait, Dannick, slide over to the side for a minute," Bellatrix said.

Dannick moved over, revealing a carving on the Devil. In the Devil's mouth, there was a key. She tried to remove it, but it was stuck.

"Hey Graham, can you help me with this?" She asked.

I noticed the key after refocusing my sleepy eyes for a minute. I was starting to zone out. I went up to the wall where the carving was and grabbed the key. I pulled it as hard as I could but had no luck. Just then Jackson and Rosette came around the bend.

"Hey Jax, can you help out here?" I asked.

"Sure buddy, what's up?" He asked

"There's a key in the mouth of this Devil. I want that key," I said.

"Say no more," Jackson said.

Jackson came over to where it was and reached his left hand into the mouth. He grasped it and pulled as hard as he could. Nothing. Then he put his feet on the wall and pulled as hard as he could and the key detached. Jackson fell on the ground.

"I never knew that," I said.

"What's that?" He asked as he stood up and dusted himself off.

"That you were a lefty," I replied.

"Oh yeah, all the smartest people are Graham," Jackson began, "To be honest though brother, I'm not a lefty for 'everything'," he said as he winked at me and laughed.

"Oh, I really didn't need to know that," I said.

Rosette laughed.

"I don't understand," Bellatrix said.

"Nevermind. It's not important. Now, what about the Aquarius part? Have any of you seen anything?" I asked.

Jackson and Rosette shook their heads.

"Alright. Wait, where are Jean and Larisa?" I asked.

Just then we heard them call out to us. We followed the voices until we were on top of a rock with them.

"What is it guys?" I asked.

"Look down mon frere," Jean said.

I looked down and saw a spring below us. We couldn't tell how deep it went. The other case must be down there, I thought.

"Alright guys, I'll be back," I said as I started taking my clothes off.

"Wait, what are you doing?" Rosette asked.

"What do you mean? I'm diving down there and getting this so we can figure out where to go next and maybe just maybe get some sleep along the way," I said.

"Yeah, but Newsdon, I'm the swimmer. I'll go," Rosette said.

"Are you sure?" Jackson asked.

"I'll be fine," Rosette said as she started taking her clothes off.

"So that's what a woman looks like?" Larisa asked as she blew Rosette a kiss.

Rosette laughed and tossed her hair to the side.

"I'll be back in five," Rosette said as she dove into the water and disappeared into a tiny dot.

We sat up there waiting for her to come back. We asked Bellatrix who she was and how come she knows so much about Bulgaria. She told us that she was recently divorced, no kids, abusive ex-husband. She was a tour guide and studied the history of Bulgaria, but in all her time doing all of that, she never thought there was a hidden code permeating through it. She was excited to be with us and she had heard of me. One of her friends had my book series as it had been translated. She admitted that she hadn't read them but was planning on them and would even like me to sign a set for her when this was all done. She told us it was a good thing that this all happened on a Friday, because she was off the weekend and had to be back at work on Monday. She wasn't sure if she was going to go back though, because what if the man with the gun was waiting there, he would certainly recognize her. Just then Rosette resurfaced.

"I need the key," she said.

"Why didn't you bring it up here so we could open it?" I asked.

"No, you don't understand. There's a room down there, I can see it. There's a vault down there that leads to a room underground. I can't make out what's in there exactly, but I just know it's there," she said.

"How deep is the water?" I asked.

"Not very deep, but it's curvy. Do you want to come with me?" She asked.

"Yeah," I said. I was already half naked from before.

"OK guys, we'll be back," Rosette said as she grabbed the key from Jackson, grabbed my hand and jumped into the water.

The water was surprisingly warm considering it was the beginning of spring. It was also pretty clear. I followed Rosette down a pathway and came up to the lock. She put the key in and turned, the door opened. The water drained into a middle room, and we closed the door behind us as quickly as we could. I looked at the floor. This place was ancient.

"Alright, what do you want to bet that this key opens that door also?" Rosette asked as she squeezed the water out of her hair.

"Let's try it," I said.

Rosette went up to the door that looked like a giant bank vault with the wheel. She put the key in, and the door swallowed it.

"Well, that's unexpected," I said.

I grabbed the wheel and spun it, then pulled it open with all my strength. The latch opened, and we were inside.

I reached over to the table and grabbed a candle. There was a pack of matches nearby. I lit the candle, and it illuminated the room a bit. We saw other candles, so one by one we lit them up until the whole room was lit.

The room was exquisite. Very well furnished and in the middle of the room, there was a glass encasing with a block of wood in it. I took a closer look.

"This is a spell," I said.

"What do you mean?" Rosette asked.

"This wood is made out of a Holly tree," I said.

"So what?" she asked.

"Druids used to make their magic wands out of the Holly tree. It's how they cast spells on people. Remember, spells are where the word spelling comes from. It also lives today casting more spells on the people?" I said.

"What do you mean? The Holly tree?" she asked.

"No, the Holly wood of the tree. It's why we have Hollywood. They cast their spells on people," I said.

"Fascinating," Rosette said as she turned and coughed up some water.

"You ok girl?" I asked.

"Yeah fine, I just swallowed some water, that's all," she said.

I opened the glass encasing and pulled out the brick of wood. There was writing all over it, but it was too dark where we were to see.

"Let's get out of here," I said.

"Right behind you," Rosette said.

"No. Actually, right in front of me. I don't know where I'm going," I advised.

"Follow me then," she said.

We left the room and got to the latch.

"OK, when I open this, it's going to send us back and the water will rush in, so we really need to swim against it," she said.

"Understood," I said.

"On three. THREE!" she said.

I hate when she does that. The door opened and water started flooding in, we fought against it and made our way out of the tunnel. I followed her as we twisted and turned and made our way back up to the surface. After a minute or so, we broke the top of the water.

"Here guys, let me help you," Jackson said as he grabbed both of us and lifted us both out of the water by himself. "We were getting worried about you."

"We're fine, I said as I turned to Rosette. She nodded.

"What did you guys find?" Larisa asked.

"This," I said as I handed them the block of wood.

"I can't really make out what this says, it's still a little too dark our here," Dannick said.

"That's fine, we have time. Let's just go find a place to crash and figure this out later," I said.

"Bellatrix, do you know a hotel around here?" Jean asked.

"As a matter of fact, I do. I stay there from time to time when I come back from visiting Greece," she said.

We all got in the car; Jackson blasted the heat for us. Jean was still a little out of it from the news he got earlier. We made our way about 10 minutes down the road, turned down a side street, turned onto a main road and then after a minute or two, turned into a hotel.

"This is more like a hostel, than a hotel," Bellatrix advised.

"That's fine," I said.

We made our way inside. Jean tried to pay in cash, but they wouldn't take it, so Bellatrix used her credit card. We all got into our separate rooms, and I passed out on the bed exhausted, not even knowing who was in bed next to me. I didn't know I was going to have a shocker of an email in my mailbox at the time. Story of my life.

There are two ways to conquer and enslave a nation. One Is by the sword. The other is by debt. —John Adams

Chapter Thirty

I woke up and checked my email. I had a letter from the President.

Dear Graham,

Things are not what they seem here. There has been an attempt on my life. Ever since you've found the 'greater' gold and released it onto the world, the markets behind the scenes have been chaotic. Countries have decided to stop using the Petrodollar for oil and some have decided to move to a Gold standard. In the past, whenever this happened to a President, behind the scenes they manufactured a war to get the leader out and install a puppet regime that would keep this going. You've changed things fundamentally and now all the countries money's are on a freefall about to collapse. This has angered those who are in charge of everything. Those who you're after right

now. It's always been about the money, every decision ever made. That's why I reached out to you. You've helped your country out so much in the last few years, that you were the only one who I could turn to. I am too high profile and can't order their arrest, it would cause a World War. They still own the media and much of society.

I had been poisoned, but the poison didn't work. Someone put arsenic in my diet coke, but luckily the diet coke was spoiled so I only had a sip. I NEED you to find these people that run everything and take them out, for the good of your country.

Forever grateful,
President Rand Dotplum

I finished reading this to everyone as we got ready to leave for the day. We still needed to figure out the last code on the Holly block. But we didn't want to stay at the hotel anymore.

We got into the van and started down the street when a SUV cut us off and slammed on the brakes. Jean slammed on the brakes, and I hit my head on the seat in front of me. I was disoriented for a few. Just then a man got out of the passenger side with a gun. Jean hit the gas and rammed the car, knocking the man over. We sped down the road.

"Jesus, what the hell was that?" I asked.

"The man is back," Bellatrix.

"How do you know it's him?" Dannick asked.

"I saw him as we passed by them," Bellatrix said.

Just then we were rear ended by the SUV.

"Where's the gun?" Bellatrix asked.

Jackson handed it over to her.

She opened the window and stuck herself out halfway. She fired a few rounds at them, which cracked the window. We couldn't tell if they were hit. Just then, the man in the front seat pulled out a shotgun and aimed it at us.

"Get down!" Bellatrix said.

We all ducked down as a shell blew through our back window, shattering it into a million pieces.

"Get us out of here Jean!" I yelled.

"This van is a piece of shit; I can't go much faster!" He yelled back.

We were chased for a few miles until we turned down a road, trying to lose them. They followed suit. After a mile or so, we saw what looked like a hospital.

"Pull in there!" Rosette yelped.

Jean pulled in, put the car in park and we all got out of the car. We ran towards the gate, which was locked.

"Climb the fence," Jackson said as he hoisted Rosette above his head, and one by one launched us to the top of the fence. Finally, he climbed over. We ran to the entrance of the Hospital, but it was boarded up. Jackson kicked a door in, and we ran inside while bullets whizzed past us.

We ran down the hallways of this abandoned hospital.

"Guys, split up," I said.

As we ran, Rosette, Larisa, Bellatrix, Jean, and Jackson ran in one direction and made their way up the stairs. Dannick and I continued to run down the hallway.

"STOP!" The man shouted.

We turned the corner, opened a door and got in.

"Great, this is a fucking linen closet," Dannick said.

"What's that smell?" I asked.

We looked down on the floor and there was aged smeared blood all over the place.

"I WILL FIND YOU!" The man shouted down the hall.

"What are we going to do?" Dannick said as he grabbed two KN95 masks from the top of the pile of linens. We put them on.

"I have no idea, just let me think a minute," I said.

"We might not have that kind of time," Dannick replied.

I analyzed our environment. There was a bucket and a mop, cleaning supplies everywhere and a vase with dead flowers in them. Carnations. Not a good sign.

"IF YOU COME OUT NOW, WE WON'T KILL YOU!" A voice shouted as we heard a shotgun cock.

One by one we heard the man kick doors in and go into the room. He was getting closer.

"Any ideas?" Dannick asked.

"Make a run for it?" I asked.

"We won't both make it," Dannick replied.

I looked at the chemicals on the floor. Suddenly, I had an idea.

"Tighten your nosepiece on your mask. This is going to burn your eyes," I said.

"YOU GO THAT WAY, I'LL STAY ON THIS SIDE!" One of the men said.

"COME OUT COME OUT WHEREVER YOU ARE!" The other man said as he blasted his shotgun at a door.

"What are you doing?" Dannick asked.

"Give me that bleach," I said.

Dannick handed me the bleach. I grabbed the vase and threw the flowers on the floor. I filled the vase halfway with bleach.

"Hand me that acetone," I said.

"The what?" Dannick asked.

"Jesus Dannick, the nail polish remover," I said.

"Why do they have nail polish remover here?" Dannick asked.

"It helps with removing nail polish," I said in a condescending tone.

"Chill, I'm just wondering," he said.

"It's for diabetics mostly. You remove nail polish. The nail bed when pressed down turns white in healthy people. It tells a lot about blood flow," I said.

He handed it to me. I opened it and filled the vase up with it.

"What is that?" Dannick asked.

"Hand me one of those towels," I replied.

Dannick handed me a towel. I soaked it in the concoction.

"This is a chloroform bomb," I said.

We sat in silence for a moment or two. Finally, we heard the man's boots at our door.

"Duck down," I whispered.

The man shot a round through the door and kicked the door open.

As soon as he was visible, I threw the vase at him as hard as I could. It exploded on his chest and went all over his face. He dropped his gun and put his hands up to his eyes.

"What did you just do to me?" He angered.

We watched as he slowly started to stumble, then fell onto the floor. I picked up the gun, just as the other man turned around and fired two rounds center mass at him. He dropped the shotgun and hit the floor dead. Dannick and I walked over to him and picked him up and brought him into the linen closet. We then dragged the other man, the one who had been after us for all time into the closet as well. We shut the door and stood the shotgun up under the door, wedging them inside.

"IT'S SAFE, COME DOWN!" I yelled up the stairwell.

After a moment of silence, we heard footsteps, and everyone came downstairs. Jackson holding an IV needle and a syringe.

"Really Jax, that's what you were going with?" I asked.

"I work with what I have. I have to protect the ladies," he said.

Jackson looked at the blood on the floor, then at the shotgun wedging the door closed. He dropped the syringe and the needle.

"What did you do?" Jackson asked as he walked towards us. When he got to the door he started to stumble.

"Jackson step back," I said as I motioned everyone to stay back.

"What did you do?" Rosette asked.

"Chloroform bomb," I replied.

"Do I even want to know how you know that?" Larisa asked.

Dannick and I took our masks off and left them on the floor.

"This place is abandoned for miles. By the time anyone finds them, they'll be dust," I said as I handed the gun over to Jackson.

"Now we have two," Bellatrix said.

"Yes we do," I replied.

We made our way down the hall and out the hospital. We got into the van, but just to be safe, Jackson slashed their tires.

"Now can we figure out where we have to go?" Jean asked.

I pulled out the Holly cube.

"Get us out of here first Jean," I replied.

"Right away," he said.

We made our way down the road again looking for a nice place to stop.

Wrong does not cease to be wrong because the majority share in it. —Leo Tolstoy

Chapter Thirty-One

"What do you mean locked in a closet in an abandoned hospital?" The man in the dark suit shouted as he looked at his phones text message.

He thought about it for a few minutes then wrote back that there would be someone sent there to take care of it. A minute later he received a text message that said thank you. Little did the man in the closet know that the person being sent there was to kill him and tie up loose ends. The news had been reporting that there were shootings and car chases at two of the caves, and this man had become a liability. Pretty soon it wouldn't matter anymore as he would be dead. The man in the dark suit sat back in his seat in the church and lit up a cigar. Graham and his friends were coming for him, and it didn't seem like there was much that he could do about it. He had already blown up their plane, sent people to kill him and they keep getting away. He was starting to realize how others before him have failed. These kids were incredibly slippery. It's fine though, he thought to himself. He did have a final contingency plan to make this all go away. In the meantime, he was trying to figure out a way with heightened security around the President since the poisoning, how he would be able to have him killed. It did occur to him that it wouldn't matter though, because the new Vice President would have been brought to speed on everything, and he was incredibly loyal to the President. If anything happened to President Dotplum, the Vice President would continue his work. This wasn't like the old days when a President was popular, and he'd pick a Vice President appointed by the council. President Lyndon Johnson came to mind. When Kennedy tried to execute order 11110, to print money and was killed, the first thing Johnson did was kill that motion. The very first thing he did. Nowadays, things were changing.

The man in the dark suit walked out of the Church with his cigar and made his way down the road. He was going to comfort himself by seeing the server room again. Truth is, where he was located there wasn't shit to do. It was always cold, and everything seemed abandoned. The man started thinking about his contingency plan. It was a long shot, but nobody would see it coming. What was an absolute at this point was that Graham Newsdon and all his friends have to die. He had their credit cards and passports flagged, so if they got wind of where he was located, he could track the flight coming in and potentially have it shot down in the sky. Lord knows there was no way to take a boat to him. It was all a waiting game at this point, one that the man hated, but he would be ready whenever something happened.

Those who do not believe in astrology have simply not studied the matter. —Sir Isaac Newton

Magic is so connected with astrology that anyone who professes magic without astrology accomplishes nothing. —Agrippa

Chapter Thirty-Two

"Alright guys, let's figure out this thing," I said as I looked at the cube.

A misnamed land craters the Mother of the Sea. Aquarius, Virgo, Pisces, Ursa Major and Ursa Minor are housed together. Not far stands a Church of Our Savior where everything is run from.

We looked at the code.

"This doesn't make any sense," I said.

"What do you mean?" Dannick asked.

"Yeah Newsdon, what gives?" Rosette asked.

"Each Zodiac sign is considered a house. Aquarius and Pisces are connecting signs, Pisces and Virgo are opposing signs and Ursa Major and Ursa Minor span a few houses. This makes no sense at all," I said. I took a CBD joint out of my pocket and lit it, my hands slightly shaking.

"Graham, can I talk to you for a second?" Rosette asked.

Never a good sign when she doesn't call by last name.

"Yeah," I said as I got out of the van and walked down the road with her.

"How are you doing bubbala?" She asked.

"Fine I guess," I said.

"You did what you had to do back at the hospital to survive. If you hadn't shot that man, we'd all be dead right now, you do realize that right?" she said.

"Yeah, I know. I mean, I remember when I dropped the pyramid on Marshall how I felt, but this was different," I said.

"How so?" She asked genuinely concerned.

"I don't know, it just feels different," I said.

"Well look, if you ever want to talk, I'm always here for you," Rosette said.

"I appreciate that," I said back to her. I was really starting to miss Hannah and my little man at this point. Although if Hannah was with us, I don't think she could handle it the way everyone else did. She's a mother now, and a damn fine one at that. James had been her top priority for years now and I loved her for that. Still, I yearned for their company.

"You almost done with that thing?" Rosette asked.

"Yeah," I said as I dropped the half smoked joint on the floor and stomped it out. We made our way back to the van.

"What do you think they mean by misnamed land?" Jean asked me.

"I mean I would think Iceland, right? Because it's all green?" Larisa said.

"Yeah, but it could also be Greenland because," I said and paused.

Everything came into focus. I understood every-thing. I had a flashback to Blur Slanders on TV.

The President of the United States tried to buy Greenland and was laughed out of the media for it, but we know what the deal really is, don't we folks. The Greenland Theory is real.

"Guys, I know where we're going," I said.

"What do you mean?" Bellatrix asked.

"Have you ever heard of the Greenland Theory?" I asked.

They all shook their head.

"The Greenland Theory says that the Roman Empire faked its own death 720 so odd years ago and now com-mands and controls all nations through its primary proxy state of Switzerland which is where the CIA is based. Formed in 1300 AD. The notion that Greenland is mostly covered in ice and snow are colossal hoaxes so Rome can Survive. President Dotplum must have known about this. Remember when he publicly stated that he wanted to buy Greenland and the media laughed at him? I think he knew, and that's why he was poisoned. The capital of the Roman Empire was in Babylon or modern-day Rome Italy and then was moved to Constantinople modern-day Istanbul Turkey. The true capital was moved to Thule which is in Greenland," I finished.

"Why Switzerland?" Jean asked.

"Think about it. The CIA is home to Switzerland. The Swiss Guard guards the Pope. The Swiss army is always neutral. They last fought in 1847. They slid and operated under the radar for all this time. Larisa, see if you can find anything about the Mother of the sea in Greenland," I advised.

"On it," Larisa said as she went to her laptop.

"I'm telling you guys, this is the heart of everything. This is where everything operates out of. I can't believe the rumors of the conspiracy theory are true. They truly are running things out of Greenland, we just need to know where," I said.

"Got something," Larisa said.

"Do tell," I replied.

"There's a statue called Mother of the Sea in a town called Nuuk," she replied.

"That's where we have to go y'all. Go figure, a town called Nuuk. As in Nukes run the world at this point," I finished.

"How are we going to get there? We don't have a plane, they blew it up earlier, and I'm sure they're flagging our credit cards," Jackson said.

I sat and thought for a minute, until Jean spoke up.

"We're near Greece, right?" He asked.

Bellatrix nodded.

"My father cosigned me on a few accounts when I was younger. We have an account at a major bank in Greece," Jean said.

"There's no way to take a boat there, it's pretty locked tight. They just don't run there," Larisa said.

"That's fine," Jean began, "We can take out cash from one of my father's accounts and pay for a chartered flight," Jean said.

We looked at each other. "That might work," I said.

"I have a strange feeling that time is of the essence," Jackson said.

"Jean, do you want me to drive?" I asked.

"No, it's best if they see me there get out of the car. There's a secret parking lot underground for high rollers so they don't have to bring money or whatever out onto the street. Larisa, please get me directions and also a quote for a chartered plane," Jean said as he started the car.

I turned to Bellatrix. "You know, you don't have to come with us, you've done more than enough so far," I said.

She looked out the window, then turned back to me, "I want to see this through, if you'll let me. Maybe I can figure out why everything is going wrong in this world," she said.

"Alright, Jean let's go," I said.

"It's a few hours' drive," he said as he put the car in drive, and we took off down the street.

My mind raced back to everything that we have been through from the beginning. The fact that there's a chance this might all end soon gave me the adrenaline rush I needed to keep going.

What the herd hates the most is the one who thinks differently. It is not so much the opinion itself, as the audacity of wanting to think for themselves. Something they do not know how to do. —Anonymous

Chapter Thirty-Three

"Yes, I'm here, can you put the code in and let me down?" Jean said into Larisas phone.

All of a sudden, the giant metal gate opened, and we made our way down the windy parking lot to the bottom. Jean parked in a spot and got out of the car.

"Wait here, I won't be long," Jean said as he made his way inside.

"Why 365?" Bellatrix asked.

"What?" I replied.

"Why 365 days in a year. Why not 360?" She asked.

"As far as I know it goes back to Thoth who was credited as the inventor of the 365-day calendar. Supposedly he won the extra five days by gambling with the moon which was then known as labet in a game of dice for 1/72 of its light. 360/72 is 5. Also 72 is a degree in the precession of the equinox that shifts, and non-ironically, the average lifespan of a male," I finished.

"What about females?" Larisa asked.

"I believe it's 77-79," I replied.

"Why?" She asked.

"I always thought it was a male self-defense mechanism to get out of marriage," I said.

"Shut up Graham," Jackson said as he punched me in the arm. "It's probably due to the manual labor throughout life that takes its tolls on men."

"So, how much does this private charter want to go there?" Rosette asked.

"A quarter mil," Larisa said.

"Wait, are you telling me that Jean is going to walk out of that bank with a quarter million dollars?" I asked.

"I'm sure it's not duffel bags of money Graham. It's probably bonds or something," Larisa advised.

We talked for a little while longer until finally we heard the door open behind us.

"Let us know if we can ever be of help to you again Mr. Solex. I'm terribly sorry about your father," A man in a suit said.

"Thank you so much," he said as he shook his hand. Jean then made his way back to the van, opened the door and tossed a manilla envelope to Larisa.

"There's a quarter million in this?" Larisa asked.

"Three hundred thousand. I took out an extra fifty. I was able to make sure they would keep our names off the manifest," Jean said.

"So nobody knows we're heading to Nuuk?" Bella-trix asked.

"I mean I keep looking behind my shoulder expecting the cop with the gun to be here, but nothing, so yeah, it would seem that way," Jean said.

"I put in the directions to the airport baby," Larisa said.

"Thanks," Jean said as he pulled the car into reverse and got out of the spot, then threw it into drive and we made our way up the winding road. We had about a two-hour drive.

We all took little cat naps which felt like 20 seconds. When I awoke, we were at the airport.

"OK guys, let me do the talking," Jean said as he took the envelope and made his way to the men in suits standing on the runway. He shook their hands and handed it over. He kept pointing at the money and then pointing at our van. One of the men motioned for us to come. Jackson jumped in the driver's seat and put the car in drive. We slowly rolled up to the men and parked.

"And what do you want us to do with this vehicle Mr. Solex?" One of the men asked.

'Torch it, get rid of it so nobody will ever find it again," he said.

"Very well. Welcome all! Your plane is fueling up. You have a flight to Greenland scheduled. Please board the plane. There are refreshments inside. Make your-selves at home," the man said as he turned around and waved the other men to come with him.

We walked up to the stairs of the plane and began ascending. After a moment or two, we were in the pri-vate plane. We all took our seats. Bellatrix took her purse and opened it up. She pulled out two guns.

"Wait a minute, what are you doing?" Jackson asked.

"Relax, I wasn't about to leave them with the car. Who knows what we'll find once we're there, no?" She asked as she handed one of them over to me.

I looked down at it. It was the same gun that I had shot the man with the shotgun with. I checked it. There were four bullets left.

"How many do you have in yours?" I asked Bella-trix.

"Six," she replied.

"Well, that's a relief. Let's hope there isn't an army there," I said as I put the gun behind my back and tucked it into my pants.

The plane finished fueling, and before long, we were in the sky. It had been a little while since we took a pri-vate jet. Not going to lie, I understand why people buy them.

It wasn't a very long flight. Well, in the scheme of previous flights we have been on. Before we knew it, we were on an icy runway in Greenland.

"When you're done here with whatever you came to do, radio me and I'll set the plane for a flight to wherever you want to go," the pilot said.

"I don't understand," I said.

"You don't think I just bought us a one way did you, Graham?" Jean asked.

"Yeah, I guess I didn't think that through," I said.

"We need to find this statue. Larisa, can you triangulate where we are and where the statue is?" Dannick asked.

"Working on it," she said.

We got out of the plane and walked down the road. There were cars lined up. When we came to a big SUV, Jackson motioned us back, punched the window in, unlocked the car and then started to wire it on. After a minute or two of fumbling around while we were keeping lookout, the car started.

"Alright guys, get in," Jackson said.

We all piled in.

"Sorry about the window guys, I know it's cold," Jackson said as he blasted the heat.

"Got it," Larisa said as she gave the address to Jackson. It was only 20 minutes away.

We parked the car and got out. We looked around for the clue. After fanning out and looking for 20 minutes, we were unable to find anything. We finally met up back at the car. That's when Dannick saw it.

"What's that?" Dannick asked.

"What's what?" I asked in return.

"That, in the water.

A misnamed land craters the Mother of the Sea. Aquarius, Virgo, Pisces, Ursa Major and Ursa Minor are housed together. Not far stands a Church of Our Savior where everything is run from.

We started making our way to the statue. The water had receded, so we were able to walk on the wet land and make our way to it.

"There it is. The mother, Virgo, the man next to her, Aquarius. The two fish, Pisces. The Bear and her cub," I said.

"How do you know it's a man? We can't really tell," Rosette asked.

I walked around to the back. His balls were hanging out.

"That's how," I said.

"So there should be a Church somewhere," I said trailing off as I looked around.

There we saw it. Within walking distance. A bright Red Church with a statue on the outside.

"The Church of Our Savior," Jackson said.

We started our walk over to it. After about 15 minutes, we pulled up at front. Jackson went to the door and opened the door.

Wisdom is given to no man until he asks for it.
—Manly P Hall

Chapter Thirty-Four

I took a step into the Church, leading my friends behind me. It was a gorgeous small church. Red carpet, light blue colors all around. A silver statue of Jesus on the back wall, art of angels all over the place. I slowly walked down the red carpet. About halfway down, there was a rather large table, full of lit candles. A jar of oil sat between it.

"Graham Newsdon I suppose," a man in a dark suit said to me.

"Who are you?" I asked.

"Sit," he replied to us.

We all stood there.

"Please sit," he said as he pulled out a gun and aimed it at us.

I pulled out my gun from behind him and aimed it at him. As did Bellatrix.

"Well, I seem to be outnumbered here. Alright," he began as he put the gun away, "stand if you will," he finished.

"Who are you?" I asked again.

The man pulled out a cigar from his pocket and cut the tip off. Then he gently picked it up off the floor and put it on the large table. He took one of the candles and lit his cigar, blowing vanilla smoke towards us.

"My name is Lash Sawbuck," the man replied.

"As in Lash from the Worlds Earnest Foundation?" I asked.

The man nodded. "Very good Graham. I knew you had to be smart to get this far. Unfortunately, this is as far as you will get," he advised.

"So, everything is true, the World is run through Greenland? Through you?" I asked.

"Ever since the elites went underground before the Tesla machine in Yellowstone, correct. I am in charge of everything on Earth. I'm the top of the top. I control the money for the Schrodhilts, I control the war, what countries borrow what money? It's all run through me," Lash said.

"I don't understand. What's the point of all of this?" I asked.

Lash Sawbuck puffed on his cigar.

"Graham, you have to understand this. People doing more than you will never put you down. It's always the people doing less. Aren't you sick and tired of all your haters online discrediting your work that has been kept secret for thousands of years just because they don't understand it or are too deep in their religion? Christ I mean, you've been shot for it. Haven't you ever wanted to just hang it all up and live a peaceful life?" Lash asked me.

I thought about what he asked of me, then thought about what he was implying.

"What are you asking of me?" I asked.

Lash jumped up out of his seat and clapped his hands together.

"Walk away from all of this. What is it you desire? A private Island? Never to pay taxes again? Enough money to put your next twenty generations of your lineage through school and life? Beautiful women around you at all times? Honestly Graham, the world could be yours, if you just walk away from this all right now," Lash said.

I sat and thought about it and looked at my friends.

"What about them?" I asked.

"Them too. We can open an offshore account for each of you and drop a billion dollars into each one of them. Graham, you have to understand, the world needs order. It needs to be run by someone. Anarchy is never the answer. Look at history. From the beginning there have always been kings and queens. A senate of elected people to govern. Everyone has to answer to someone higher than them. It keeps them in line," Lash said.

"Who do you answer to?" I asked.

"At first it was the Pope, hundreds of years ago until the Battle of Waterloo event happened with the Schrodhilts. They installed my family to be the failsafe in case things went out of whack. Someone always needs to be in charge Graham. But you know this. You know that the Church's time is up being out of the age of Pisces now. Even if it's not in our lifetime, your own work says it! They will decline in numbers, just like the Jews did after Aries, just like the Egyptians did after Taurus. It's a New Order amongst us," Lash said.

"That's why you're opening the One World Religion Headquarters in Jerusalem," I said.

"Precisely. See, thousands of years ago, before the internet, before phones, before any form of immediate overseas communication, you could create a religion, then send people out to slaughter and convert in its name, and that was how it would get done. But now, no chance. With the internet and camera phones, everyone having an AquaStream channel, you could never organically grow a religion. Even with all the misinformation and disinformation that we pay to have people put out there to confuse people who search things online, even with owning the biggest search engines on the planet, it wouldn't work. The One World Religion Headquarters is just the thing we need to bring everyone together. You unfortunately exposed a key to it with the start of Islam through the Church. We're in the Age of Aquarius now, and it's my job to lead it," Lash said.

"But why the Central Banks? Why keep everyone in crippling debt for all eternity?" I asked.

"It keeps everyone in check. It keeps the chaos of being overpopulated in order. Religion and debt keep people focused on things so that we can run the rest," Lash said.

"We're not overpopulated, we're just overpopulated in major metropolis's," I said.

"Whatever it is, it's been very helpful to us to do things this way," Lash said.

"So, what's next?" I asked.

"Well, there is a server room about a block and a half down from here where we keep all financial loans and debts. We're going to back that up, then move to a new location. Truth be told, I fucking hate Greenland. It's always so cold. Honestly, with all the money we have in the world, why we couldn't do this from a warmer place I have no idea. Although, maybe it's to keep people from finding out. You are the first visitors I've ever had here since I started running things years ago," Lash said.

"It's never going to stop, is it? Countries will never be able to pay back their debts," I said.

"Well, every time someone tries to get off the US dollar in oil, your government sends people in to change the regime. This should make you happy as you live in the US. You're lucky. You've got an ocean across from all the war and horror in the world, and your neighbors are Canada and Mexico. Even Mexico, only does low level things like trafficking and gun and drug smuggling. Nobody's aiming nuclear weapons at you. Even if they did, you've got an East Coast with anti-missile silos to protect you. Honestly, you should count your lucky stars that you live in the US," he finished.

"When the dollar falls, it's not going to make a difference," I said.

"Then we will have a one world cryptocurrency. All money will be digital, there will be no need for central banks. That will be the next step. What I'm offering you is a chance to be a part of that. ALL OF YOU. Just get back in your van, go to the airport, go home and you will be given further instructions," he said.

"What about the President?" I asked.

"President Dotplum has been a thorn in our side for many years. Honestly, it's embarrassing that you can't poison someone so easily anymore. He will have to go. The Vice President who's loyal to him that he just selected will have to go as well, and another long-term

Senator will be put in his place to keep the system going," Lash said.

I sat and thought about this for a few minutes. Then I turned to my friends, and we started discussing.

"Don't mind me, take all day," Lash said.

We kept talking. Honestly the thought of never having to have to worry about anything financially for our families' lives for eternity was an incredibly tempting idea. We decided against it.

"I'm sorry Mr. Sawbuck. You know, it's tempting to think about how you're offering us paradise, unending money, security and protection. All of us. But it's just that pesky thing of conscience that we have. I'm afraid we're not going to be able to take you up on this," I said as I stood up.

"I'm very sorry to hear that, Graham. You know, they say you're hard to kill. I don't see how that's possible and how so many people failed before me," Lash said as he took his gun out and aimed it at me.

Immediately, I reacted and took the gun out of my back and aimed it at him. Bellatrix did the same.

"It looks like you're outnumbered Lash," I said.

Lash, keeping his gun aimed at me started to laugh, and I mean howl. After a minute or two he stopped, wiped tears away from his eyes, looked over at me, then at Bellatrix and cocked his head to the side.

All at once, Bellatrix took two steps towards him, then turned around and aimed the gun at me.

"See in movies, we call this, the 'twist,' " Lash said laughing.

"Bellatrix, what are you doing? Get back here," Jackson said.

"I'm sorry guys. I really enjoyed getting to know all of you, really. I couldn't have gotten here without you. I've got a lot of struggling family in Bulgaria. I have a young son, cousins in poverty. Why couldn't you just take the deal?" She asked as she cocked her gun.

All at once it hit me.

"Bellatrix Rigel. Is that even your name?" I asked.

"What do you mean?" She asked.

"Bellatrix and Rigel are two of the three stars in Orion's Belt. Were you part of the great Astrological deception all along?" I asked.

Bellatrix laughed.

"So, the cop that was following up the entire time, he wasn't one of you?" I asked starting to put the pieces of the puzzle together.

"Of course he wasn't," Lash advised.

I picked up her purse that was on the row behind me and pulled out her phone. I went through the text messages and emails.

"It was you that was giving him our constant up-dates?" I asked.

"Again, Graham, just take the deal," Bellatrix said.

I looked at them, both pointing their guns at me. I looked back behind me to my friends who were with me throughout this journey. I thought about the people that we have picked up and lost along the way, I thought back to NP. A sudden thought came into my head that I would be seeing him real soon.

"What's it going to be Graham?" Lash asked as he pointed the gun to the side of me and fired a round. It hit one of the candles which exploded onto the floor and started a small fire. Bellatrix quickly jumped on it and stomped it out.

"I'm sorry guys, but I just can't be a part of this," I said as I handed the gun over to Jackson and turned to face them.

"This will be my greatest regret that I couldn't convince the great Graham Newsdon to join us and make the new Age the best one yet," he said as he re-aimed his gun to me and cocked it. I closed my eyes. I heard the gun go off but get stuck. I opened my eyes and saw something I never thought I'd see. A white butterfly came in across the room and fluttered up to him, landing on the barrel of his gun.

"You know, in the shamanic cultures, synchronici-
ties are recognized as signs that you are on the right
path," I said as all at once in one fell swoop, I picked up
the pitcher of oil and tossed it at Lash, then with my
other hand I picked up a candle and threw it at him. The
candle shattered and ignited the oil that covered him. He
went up like a Christmas tree. I then spun around and
grabbed the table and lifted it up off the ground, knocking all the candles to the floor. The entire place went up
in smoke and flames.

"Run!" I screamed as we all made our way to the
front door. We exited the Church as I gave one look
back. Bellatrix was trying to put Lash out with a blanket.
We shut the door to the Church, and Jackson found a
giant two by four on the ground. He wedged it into the
door handles, locking them in. After a moment or two
we heard and saw the door trying to swing open, but the
two by four kept it closed. After another moment we
heard a blood curdling scream, then there was just the
silence of the fire.

"Guys, we have to find that server room and take it
out!" I said as we looked down the road. There was only
one building that was about a 5-minute walk. We made
our way in there. There was a guard.

"Hey you! You're not allowed to be in here!" He
said as he aimed his gun at us. Jackson pulled out his

gun and aimed it at his head. Jackson then walked up to the man and collected his gun, then pistol whipped him, knocking him out onto the ground.

We made our way down the corridor, turned the corner, and were faced with what basically amounted to a warehouse with servers.

"Larisa, do your thing," I said.

"Got it," She replied as she walked aisle by aisle, disabling them all. Then she walked back to the bathroom in the corner, filled up a giant garbage can with water, and dragged it out.

"A little help Jackson," she said.

"Right," he replied.

The two of them methodically, one by one, sprayed water onto each server. They started to cackle with electricity. After refilling the water and doing this for about 45 minutes, they were done.

"Come on guys, we need to go back to that church," Dannick said.

We left the server room, which without the heat generated from them, and the cooling system still on, was an icebox. We went back down the hallway, Jackson picked up the man on the floor and put him in his chair. We walked outside and back down the street.

We got to the Church and Jackson removed the two by four. We opened the door and the smoke bellowed through. There were only a few small fires scattered amongst the rubble. We walked inside and saw two charred bodies on the floor. One was Bellatrix as we recognized her clothing, the other was Lash, cigar still in his mouth. We felt their pulse, and they were both long gone. A wave of relief came over me.

"Guys, I think it's finally done. All of it," I said.

I turned back to them, and they all seemed relieved. We made our way back to the van, got in and started heading straight to the airport.

"Larisa, give me your computer real quick; I want to email the President and explain to him everything," I said.

Larisa handed it over, secured with a VPN and opened an encrypted email address for me. I spent the next hour typing the President an email of everything we had encountered. What we had been through, what it led us to. Who was really running things and what ended up happening to them as well as the server room. I hit send and closed the computer. After about 20 minutes I heard an alert from the computer. I opened it up and he responded. Jesus, does this guy ever sleep? He told me that he was incredibly proud of us and not to get on any plane, he would send one for us. He said he had big plans for me, as he would be addressing the na-tion in a week and wanted us there.

We waited at the airport for a few hours until a small private jet showed up. A man in a suit got out of it and walked down the steps. He walked over to us and after confirming who we were, he motioned for us to follow him into the plane, which we did. He congratulated us for doing something that nobody in the history of the World in the last 300 years has been able to do. He told us that the President told him that big things were coming. Although he was thankful for everything, he made Jackson give him his gun, which Jackson laughed about. After about half an hour, we were into the air and the night.

"What sparked your power move back there?" Jackson asked me.

"Honestly it was the white butterfly. I keep seeing those everywhere," I replied.

"Did you know that Plato's real name was Aristocles. When his father brought him to study with Socrates, the great skeptic declared that on the previous night he had dreamed of a white swan, which was an omen that his new disciple was to become one of the world's illumined," Jackson said.

"No shit," I replied.

I closed my eyes as we made our way to our homeland. I had no idea what the President had in store for us.

Beware that, when fighting monsters, you yourself do not become a monster, for when you gaze long into the abyss, the abyss gazes also into you.

—Friedrich Nietzsche

Chapter Thirty-Five

We took the flight straight into Dulles Airport. Once we got there, there was a giant SUV waiting for us. We got in and started making our way to the White House. After a short trip, we arrived at the White House and went down into the parking lot under it that most people don't know about. A secret service agent let us out, and we followed him through the White House and into the Rose Garden, where the press was already set up. They showed us to our seats. Apparently, the President had some sort of announcement to make to the American people and requested us to be there in person to see it. After about 20 minutes, he finally came out, and made his way to the podium.

"My fellow Americans. Today is a glorious day, a great day, possibly the greatest day in the history of our country. For national security concerns I can't go too deep into it, but I just wanted to share with you some changes that will be made in our administration. Firstly, under my authority, we will officially pardon Julian Assange, Edward Snowden and Ross Ulbricht. What they have done was a great service to society, as we should be held accountable for our actions, not discourage future whistleblowers from coming forward with the threat of punishment. That's my first order of business. Second, we are making daylight savings permanent. There is no need for it to get dark at 3 pm, while thousands and thousands of people suffer from seasonal depression and the lack of the Sun," he paused and took a sip of water. "Next, we have a rampant problem with Pedophilia, in literally all states of life. This is a horrific problem that finally has a solution. Your first offense will garner you 15 years in prison, whereas your second offense will result in the death penalty. There is no reason that child exploitation should be this big of a problem in this country, and yes, it really will be that simple," he concluded.

"Mr. President. Where are you getting your facts from? There isn't a pedophilia problem in our country," one reporter said.

"Sit down," the President began, "Have you ever seen a map of missing kids in the United States? Then placed a map of the cave system in the United States? They're almost identical. Also, you in the media refuse to report all these stories, the media is complicit in this.

No more. First offense, 15 years, unless it's a horrific offense where the child dies, and second offense is the death penalty. I have spoken to my people, and we feel this is the best way to address this, and I hope that my fellow countries around the world see the wisdom in it and follow suit. We will also be working with the hacker group Anonymous in order to tackle the child trafficking problem in this country.

Next, I am taking a playbook from France, our lovely French allies over the pond. Any food that isn't sold in a supermarket, MUST be given to shelters and homeless facilities. Also, there will be an initiative for us to plant fruit trees throughout our country so that people can grab them from the trees and eat them. We've tried working on the homeless problem a few years ago, but there is so much more to be done. I hope this will begin the healing of that problem.

Now, in regard to another problem in the United States. As of this moment, I am signing an executive order that bans fluoride in toothpaste as well as water. We know the damage this causes people, yet nobody has done anything about it. Well, I am. There is a miasma of health problems that can occur from a buildup of fluoride, it's time we addressed this," he finished.

"Sir, it sounds like you're taking many of your talking points from Blur Slanders. Have you had a chance to go over it with anyone?" One reporter asked.

"It's amazing to me that bettering and fighting for my country gets me labeled as what you consider a conspiracy theorist. People just don't look into this stuff. I will not answer that question as it offends me. I'm not done, however. Due to national security, I can't tell you more than this, but what I am allowed to tell you is that there was an evil faction in this world that controlled our money supply. It's why every country was in debt. Well, the constitution says that we are chartered to print money on the good faith of the people. Money backed by tangible things, unlike what the Central Banks in the World have done. This has led to taxes to pay back the money we borrow from them out of thin air. They are now trying to tax your unrealized capital gains, there is a section in the IRS playbook that says how to collect taxes a month after a nuclear explosion, we'll get to the nuclear part in a few. And now, they want to tax you for every mile you drive. The Federal reserve is at the bottom of all of this. I have spoken to allies and enemies over the past two days advising them what I was about to do and for them to follow suit with these Central Banks. Did you know that during the 1720 financial crisis, British Parliament debated a resolution for bankers to be sewn in sacks with snakes & dumped into the Thames? Well, we can't do that anymore, but we can do something about this institution that had our great President Kennedy killed for doing what I am about to do. Starting today, we are starting the Freedom One Bank of America which will print our money based on precious metals reserves. In fact, I have a special surprise for you in a short while. As Buckminster Fuller said, it is now highly feasible to take care of everybody on Earth at a higher standard of living than any have ever known. It no longer has to be you or me. Selfishness is unnecessary. War is obsolete. It is a matter of converting the high technology from weaponry to livingry. This is exactly correct. I was on the phone all day yesterday and for the last few days talking to our allies across the world, and we've decided to destroy all nuclear weapons. There is no need to keep these. Now, our military defenses will always be up as will theirs overseas, but we are edging towards a treaty which will see that a committee will oversee the destruction of all nuclear weapons. There is no reason to be living like this anymore. As I mentioned our great President Kennedy once said that he will splinter the CIA into a thousand pieces and scatter it into the winds. I intend on doing that. The CIA is only good for regime changes and starting proxy wars. There's so much lie and deception through them that I view them as their own septic entity. I am signing an executive order today to disband them. Now, if you'll excuse me, I need to take some friends on a little ride," President Dotplum said as he pointed to us. We stood up and walked to where the President was standing, and the light bulbs went off in blinding fashion. We were going to be splattered on every newspaper across the country. We walked inside the White House with the President.

"Graham my dear friend and your friends, how do you think I did out there? What did you think of my speech?" The President asked as we and secret service followed him back down to the car lot.

"I think that if I were trying to get killed, I couldn't write something that perfect for that," I said.

President Dotplum laughed.

"Graham, they already tried to get me once. They failed in spectacular fashion. I have a Vice President now who will back me up no matter what happens," he finished.

"So, when you tried to buy Greenland a little while back?" I asked.

The President stopped walking and turned to me. "I was foolish to go about it that way. I needed some people who could get to the bottom of it and take care of it for me. You and your friends have been a Godsend to this Country from the beginning. That's why I have a special treat for you lined up," he said as we continued to walk.

We made our way down to the vehicles and I got in the SUV with the President, my friends got in the one behind us.

"Where are we going?" I asked.

"You'll see," President Dotplum smiled back at me.

After a short drive I knew where we were. We stepped out at the Federal Reserve Building. There was a barricade behind us and an enormous crowd of people.

"My fellow Americans, today is a great day, when history looks back at today they'll say it's the day we took back our country and stopped poisoning our citizens, both literally and figuratively. I was going to do this myself, but I think I'll leave the honors to Graham," he said as he pulled out a remote. "Just push the button when you're ready Graham," he said.

I looked at it. There was no way this was what I thought it was.

I turned to the right and I saw a person painting a portrait of the Fed on fire and gallows out in front.

"That sucks for the 87,000 new IRS workers don't it!" A man behind me shouted.

After looking at the crowd and a large chanting of 'Push It' I did.

Little by little, the Federal Reserve building crumbled to the ground. There was massive cheering from behind us. The President shook my hand and waved my friends over. We turned around and there was a camera man there. We all smiled and took a perfect picture that I was going to get framed and hung on my wall.

"Alright Graham, it's time for you and your friends to go on a vacation. We've chartered a Jet to bring you to Boston to pack, then they will take you anywhere in the world you want to go for a vacation," the President said.

I looked at him and blinked in awe.

"It's the least we can do. Thank you for everything. I mean, everything," he said as he held his hand out for me to shake it. Which I did.

The SUV took us back to the airport and we were on a short flight to Boston. Once we landed, we went to our homes and packed. Hannah was watching the TV when I entered the house, and James ran up to me and hugged me.

"Your daddy is a hero!" Hannah squealed at James.

"I saw you on TV!" James said to me.

I hugged them both and explained to them everything that happened, even the part where we were going on a vacation.

After an hour or two of packing, everyone started calling my phone, and Jean came to pick us up in his van. We made our way to the airport.

"Where are we going to go?" I asked.

"Bora Bora!" Rosette shouted.

"Ft. Lauderdale," Dannick said.

"Cabo San Lucas," Jackson said.

"Italy," Larisa said.

Just then, I got a call from a DC number. I picked it up, it was the President.

"Hello Graham, I hope I'm not interrupting you right now," President Dotplum said.

"No not at all, we're just figuring out where we're going on vacation," I replied.

"Good for you. Listen, I don't want to worry you, but I thought you should know. By the time our people got to the Church in Nuuk, the bodies inside were gone," he said.

"What do you mean gone? Like someone took them?" I asked.

"We don't know, I just wanted to keep you posted. Have a great vacation," he said as he hung up the phone.

We got on the plane and tried to figure out where we were going to go. This was going to take a little bit. But as long as I was with my friends, I could handle anything. My name is Graham Newsdon, and I know the answer to the world's deepest secret. And now, so do you. What will you do? Will you sit on this information, or will you share it with the world?

Upcoming New Release!

Into the Rabbit Hole
The Ultimate Truth
By Micah T. Dank

The Ultimate Truth, Book Nine, the continuation of *Into the Rabbit Hole.*

For more information
visit: www.SpeakingVolumes.us

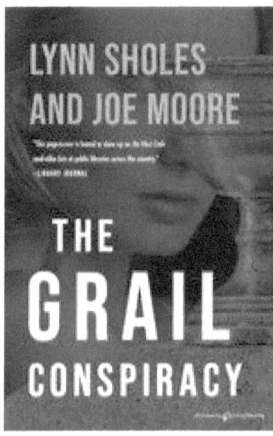
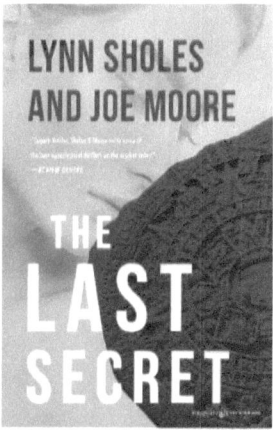